Every day she felt worse about her decision to end things with Alistair rather than better.

She had come the closest yet to caving and calling the station he was based at and asking him to contact her.

To say she was sorry, sorry, sorry and had made a ridiculous mistake.

But please, don't take that job… Oh, and can you get rid of your bike, please? And, in the interest of full disclosure, before you change your life because I ask you to, you should know I'm going to be a mess any day soon if I find out I can't get pregnant…

Their feelings couldn't survive the real world, Libby decided.

And when she got home from the shopping trip she'd pretended to be on, her mother was pacing because her father hadn't called her back.

Oh, heavens!

That would've been Libby's future if she had stayed with Alistair.

THE NURSE'S PREGNANCY WISH

CAROL MARINELLI

HARLEQUIN
MEDICAL
ROMANCE

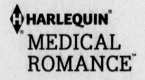

HARLEQUIN®
MEDICAL
ROMANCE™

Recycling programs
for this product may
not exist in your area.

ISBN-13: 978-1-335-73762-5

The Nurse's Pregnancy Wish

Copyright © 2023 by Carol Marinelli

For questions and comments about the quality of this book, please contact us at CustomerService@Harlequin.com.

Harlequin Enterprises ULC
22 Adelaide St. West, 41st Floor
Toronto, Ontario M5H 4E3, Canada
www.Harlequin.com

Printed in U.S.A.

Carol Marinelli recently filled in a form asking for her job title. Thrilled to be able to put down her answer, she put "writer." Then it asked what Carol did for relaxation and she put down the truth—"writing." The third question asked for her hobbies. Well, not wanting to look obsessed, she crossed her fingers and answered "swimming"—but, given that the chlorine in the pool does terrible things to her highlights, I'm sure you can guess the real answer!

Books by Carol Marinelli

Harlequin Medical Romance

Paddington Children's Hospital
Their One Night Baby

Their Secret Royal Baby
The Midwife's One-Night Fling
The Nurse's Reunion Wish
Unlocking the Doctor's Secrets

Harlequin Presents

Scandalous Sicilian Cinderellas
The Sicilian's Defiant Maid
Innocent Until His Forbidden Touch

Cinderellas of Convenience
The Greek's Cinderella Deal
Forbidden to the Powerful Greek

Visit the Author Profile page
at Harlequin.com for more titles.

CHAPTER ONE

Paramedic Alistair Lloyd knew exactly what everybody called him.

He even answered to the name at times.

For the most part it didn't bother him.

Now and then it irked.

It was cold, wet and raining in London— slushy sleet that seeped down the back of a person's neck and meant entering the very warm Accident and Emergency department caused his ears to sting just a little.

Alistair was working with Brendan today, and Brendan was extremely good-natured and very good at his job—though not quite as pedantic as Alistair.

That was the reason for his nickname: Perfect Peter.

Alistair never strayed from protocol.

Frankly, if it had been his call, Alistair would have alerted the Accident and Emergency department of London's Primary Hospital prior to the arrival of this patient. Brendan, who had been treating while Alistair was driving, had chosen not to.

'What now?'

Libby Bennett's friend Dianne, who was working in Resus, looked up from the leg she was holding as a doctor applied traction. They both saw a patient arriving on a spinal board with his head strapped down.

'I'll go,' Libby said, and then frowned. 'Who's that Brendan's working with?'

She only asked because she'd thought Brendan was rostered on with Rory.

'Perfect Peter.' Dianne rolled her eyes and got back to the leg she was holding. 'Good luck…'

Libby, who had only been working at The Primary for three weeks, was far too new to know what Dianne's roll of the eyes and rather sardonic 'good luck' meant; she was just worried about her fridge! It was being dropped off at three—the only time the driver could do it. Rory had offered to move it up the two flights of stairs to her apartment, and had roped in the older, rather portly Brendan into helping him—and now Rory wasn't here.

Still, it wasn't the patient's problem, so she made her way over and smiled down at the young man who lay on the spinal board. 'Hello, I'm Libby.'

'Marcus…'

Her new patient was a young gentleman with a clearly fractured wrist, though he was smiling and possibly appearing a little too happy, given his predicament.

'Marcus is a twenty-seven-year-old male,' Brendan said, 'who fell from the first-floor window of his flat.'

'It was an accident,' Marcus elaborated. 'We were just messing about…trying to get the best control.'

'Gaming,' Brendan further explained. 'Marcus was standing on the bed and he says he fell backwards through the closed window behind it.'

'Gaming?' Libby blinked.

It wasn't particularly relevant, but Libby wanted to engage the patient in conversation while she assessed him and decided where best he should be placed. She'd also heard the 'he says he fell' in Brendan's handover, which raised flags as to whether the patient might have jumped or been pushed.

'I never knew it could be so dangerous!'

'Obvious right wrist fracture,' Brendan continued, 'but apart from that—'

'I'm fine,' Marcus said. 'Can I get this thing off my neck?'

Marcus had been strapped to a spinal board and had on a cervical collar.

'Not just yet,' Libby said.

All precautions had been taken, Brendan told her, with a slight edge to his voice. And Libby listened as he explained the scene he had found on his arrival, and the distance the patient had fallen, and the fact that Marcus had been sitting up when they had arrived.

It really did sound like an accident that had happened while Marcus and his friend had wrestled for the gaming control, although Brendan informed her that the police had also been on scene, and they were currently speaking with the friend and would soon be coming in to interview Marcus.

There were certain standard operating procedures in place for falls, and this patient was borderline. While his fall had been broken by some bushes, the distance he had fallen was close to the cut-off that meant his injuries could be more serious than were obviously apparent. She was just coming to a decision when she glanced up at the other paramedic—the one who should have been Rory but wasn't, and whom she thought Dianne had said was

called Peter—and he silently mouthed two
words: *Long fall.*

He did it so that neither Brendan nor the patient could see, letting Libby know that he was
also concerned by the distance the patient had
fallen. He had been on scene too, after all, and
it was good to have all the information.

'Straight through,' Libby said, gesturing to
Resus, but her patient started when he saw the
red sign and realised where he was headed.

'Why am I being taken in there?'

'It's just a precaution because of how far
you've fallen,' Libby explained. 'Don't be
alarmed by all the equipment—it's just until
we know that you're stable.'

'I've only hurt my wrist, though.'

'Even so,' Libby said as they wheeled him
in, 'it's better to be cautious and get you properly seen to.'

Still Marcus objected. 'I told them I could
walk...'

'Well, it's best you don't,' Libby said as she
moved the stretcher alongside the flat Resus
bed and tried to reassure him. 'Marcus, it's best
we take all precautions. Let me worry about all
that. Believe me, I'm very good at it.' She made
him smile as they set up to move him. 'I'm a
professional worrier, in fact...'

She wasn't lying. Libby, even though she

tried her best not to, worried about almost everything!

Because, if she didn't worry enough, things tended to fall apart.

The fridge being a case in point!

Not that she was thinking about that now...

Dianne came in to assist with the move, as did a couple of others, but, glancing up, she saw Peter checking that the brakes had been secured on both beds and refusing to be rushed.

'Come on, Alistair,' Dianne chided, and Libby frowned. Hadn't Dianne just told Libby that his name was Peter?

Whatever his name was, he nodded, seemingly more in affirmation to himself that all was well than for Dianne's benefit, and then returned to the head of the stretcher. It was then that she discovered his eyes were the darkest brown.

A deep, chocolate-brown, with spiky black lashes and gorgeously arched brows. He was drenched—no doubt frozen—yet somehow Libby couldn't help but notice he still managed to look incredible. His black hair was wet from the rain, his skin pale, and he was clean-shaven. She also noted that he stood a head above everyone else, both in stature and presence.

Though their eyes met for less than a second, it was enough that Libby felt her cheeks redden.

She could blame it on many things—sliding the patient over, the heat in Resus, or the fact that she'd been racing around all morning—only it wasn't just that.

She was suddenly aware that she must look an utter fright. She'd been in full PPE for most of the morning, so her blonde curls were dark with sweat. As well as that, her hair tie had snapped on her arrival at work, so her curls were now being held back with a crepe bandage.

The heat on her cheeks would not fade, and it was actually a relief that it was Brendan who was the treating paramedic and giving the handover, as she was about to turn into one burning blush.

'What do we have?' Huba, the emergency doctor, came in as Libby set about doing her patient's observations.

'A fractured wrist,' Dianne responded a touch tartly, glancing over to Libby.

It was clear that Dianne thought she had overreacted.

In the end, there wasn't actually a chance to have a word with Brendan about her fridge, because he was being summoned by his very good-looking partner. So Libby put all thoughts of fridges and stairs completely out of her head as she called X-Ray and then dealt with Marcus, who was concerned about his friend.

'I've told the police it was an accident,' he fretted. 'Why are they questioning him?'

'Marcus, I don't know what the police are doing.' Libby was honest but firm. 'For now, let's focus on you.'

'But I'm fine. I could walk if you'd let me.'

'Libby, go and have your break,' Dianne cut in, clearly a bit miffed, because she was in charge of Resus today, and didn't think the patient needed to be in there—though she'd had to accept the decision, and since there was a bed free for him she didn't challenge it.

It was quiet for a Thursday morning.

Well, no one was allowed to say the Q-word, or comment on the fact that it was unusually Q for a Thursday, because the second they did the Bat Phone would buzz, the doors would fly open and everyone in the waiting room would simultaneously collapse—or something similar.

So for now Libby took her morning coffee break and headed to the kitchen beside the staffroom. She retrieved her cheese and biscuits from the fridge and then put her hand up to compare the height of the staffroom fridge to what she thought was the size of the gap in the wall of kitchen units at her new and exceedingly tiny studio flat.

Oh, God, even if she did somehow get it up the stairs, Libby wasn't at all sure that the fridge she was having delivered was going to fit.

'Libby!'

Brendan made her jump, and she stopped mentally measuring the fridge and watched as he speed-filled his mug with coffee—paramedics never got long between jobs.

'You're going to need to find someone else to help me with the fridge,' he said. 'I'll be there as soon as we're finished, but Rory's off sick. I've got...'

He gestured to the dark hunk behind him, who was helping himself to some biscuits. A lot of biscuits! He had three in his hand and was munching his way through them as Brendan tried to rope his colleague in to assist Libby with her fridge.

'I didn't catch your name,' Libby ventured, but instead of enlightening her he helped himself to more biscuits as Brendan explained her predicament.

'Rory agreed to move Libby's new fridge with me,' Brendan said. 'The driver's dropping it off at three and she's got no one to help her...'

'I didn't know that I was just paying for delivery,' Libby explained.

She realised that without even trying she was blinking and batting her eyelashes—her green eyes, which on a normal day cheerfully greeted everyone, were flirting of their own accord!

'But it turns out I have to arrange people to lift it. I thought the price was good value for money.'

'She paid him up-front.' Brendan laughed as he told his colleague. 'How long have you lived in London now?'

'Three weeks,' Libby said.

'It shows,' Brendan said, then turned to his partner, who Libby hadn't heard speak out loud yet. 'The thing is, now Rory's off sick and I need someone to help me lift it.'

But the man shook his head. 'I've got a physical assessment tomorrow,' he said, while dipping a biscuit in his coffee. 'I'm not hauling a fridge.'

He didn't so much as look at Libby, just denied his assistance in a deep, sexy voice, and Brendan gave Libby a helpless shrug of his shoulders, as if to show what he was up against.

'I'll find someone,' Libby said, blinking her eyelashes with disappointment now.

She didn't really know many people in London. And, given it was pouring with rain, who would want to drag a fridge up two flights of stairs?

A fridge that might not even fit when it got there.

'I'll ask around,' Libby attempted in an up-beat tone, and smiled at Brendan. 'What time do you think you'll get to mine?'

'All depends what time we get our last job. It could be quite late,' Brendan warned. 'Make sure you get someone to help me, Libby…'

'Of course.' She nodded and watched as the hungry paramedic, whose name she still didn't know, took another handful of biscuits and completely ignored both her vivid green eyes and her plight.

'We need to get going,' he told Brendan as the radio on his shoulder summoned them.

'We haven't cleared yet.'

'I have,' he said, and walked off.

'God…' Brendan sighed, screwing the lid on his mug and following his partner out. 'No rest for the wicked!'

Libby smothered a giggle as Brendan huffed off.

Whatever his name was, it was no wonder they called him Perfect Peter, Libby thought as she ate her cheese and crackers and drank a huge mug of tea.

He really was *perfect*.

Not just tall, dark and handsome, but all brooding and silent—and self-centred enough that he wouldn't help with her fridge.

Libby tended to go for that type, but she was determined—*determined*—only to date nice, safe and sensible guys from now on.

The kind of caring and thoughtful guy who was strong enough to manage a fridge. One who would gallantly put his stupid physical assessment in jeopardy for her...

And who didn't mind about her ovaries.

With a weary sigh she leant back on the chair.

Libby was, despite her bright smile and friendly nature, not having the best day. She had *finally* been contacted by her home GP regarding a gynae appointment, having been referred *ages* ago. Seriously, ages ago. In the weeks prior to the appointment she'd have to undergo blood tests, and a detailed ultrasound, but she should be able to fit the investigations in as she was going to be home in Norfolk for her mother's sixtieth birthday at around the same time.

Libby needed to text her response, and confirm the appointment time for the tests, only she hadn't yet done so.

The trouble was that she wasn't sure if she wanted to know why her periods had dropped to every two or three months—or the reason for a few other issues she'd been dealing with.

She was oddly tempted to call and tell them she'd moved, just so the investigations and appointments would be cancelled. But then she would have to start the process of finding a new GP in London, and go through all the waiting again to find out she might have fertility issues, as her GP back home had suggested.

She'd been upset by the possibility, and felt she had nowhere to turn.

That was partly due to the fact that her boyfriend at the time had been hurtful, rather than helpful, and although Libby had got rid of him quick-smart, now she felt even more alone. Her close friend Olivia hadn't been as helpful as Libby had hoped either—although in fairness she'd been pregnant herself at the time, and busy with concerns of her own. And Libby didn't want to confide in her mother, who made Libby's low-grade anxiety look like a walk in the park.

It was something she didn't want to face, but Libby knew she had to get answers.

It was just so very hard facing it alone.

Draining her cup, she put it in the sink.

'Rinse it,' Paula the ward domestic warned. 'You wouldn't leave your own cups like that—'

'Sorry,' Libby said. 'Actually, I do leave

my own cups like that at home!' She smiled at Paula as she washed and dried her mug. 'I keep meaning to get a routine, but I leave cups everywhere. Still, that's no excuse,' she said, and put away her mug.

She headed back out towards the department and bumped into Ricky, one of the porters.

'Ricky!' She beamed. 'I have a fridge being delivered this afternoon. One of the paramedics has offered to help, but not till the evening...'

'No chance,' Ricky said.

In the end, her 'long fall' patient was possibly the most willing in the department.

'I'd do it Libby,' he said, 'if I wasn't stuck here.'

Marcus had had his X-rays, been interviewed by the police, and his cervical collar had been taken off. Now he was waiting for the ortho- pods to review his wrist.

'That's very kind of you.' Libby smiled. 'It's a shame about the broken wrist...'

'I could ask my friend. He should be in soon, now that the police finally believe it was an accident.'

'There's no need for that,' Libby said, and her smile hid her sudden concern, because the formerly ruddy Marcus had gone a little pale. 'How are you doing?'

'I feel a bit sick, to be honest.'

'Okay,' Libby said, running another set of obs. 'Have you got any pain—aside from in your wrist?'

'Not really. Maybe a bit in my shoulder.'

'That's new, is it?'

His blood pressure was low and his heart rate was starting to creep up. Summoning Huba in, to reassess him, Libby lay her patient down.

'Let's increase the fluids,' Huba said, instantly concerned at his sudden decline. 'Any pain in your stomach, Marcus?' she asked as she examined his abdomen.

'Not really.'

'Okay.' Huba looked over to Libby. 'Can you page the on-call surgeon, and also the path lab, and see how the cross-match is coming along.'

'What's wrong?' Marcus asked.

'I just want to be sure that you're not bleeding internally,' Huba explained. 'Sometimes shoulder tip pain can be a sign of bleeding into the abdomen, and you're looking very pale.'

He was looking so pale, in fact, that by the time Dianne had come back from her break the surgeons were diagnosing a ruptured spleen and Marcus was being prepared for an urgent dash to Theatre.

'Good call,' Dianne said a short while later, once Marcus was in Theatre. 'I'd have had him in a cubicle.'

'I might have too,' Libby admitted, as together they wiped down the Resus bed, preparing it for its next guest. 'Perfect Peter was quite insistent that he was to be treated as a long fall.'

'Well, he was right,' Dianne said.

'Why do you call him Perfect Peter? What's his actual name?'

'Alistair.' Dianne laughed. 'We just call him that…'

'Behind his back?' Libby sighed, completely understanding his nickname—he was seriously gorgeous after all. 'I looked a right fool.'

'Sorry about that.' Dianne smiled again, then got back to discussing their patient. 'Thank goodness Marcus was able to give a full statement to the police before he went to Theatre, or his friend really would be in trouble.'

'Gosh…' Libby said, placing a fresh sheet down and a roll of paper. 'All that from gaming!'

Marcus's parents arrived then, and Libby showed them into Interview Room One, where Huba came and spoke with them. She had a lovely, calming nature, Libby thought as Huba explained what had happened.

'Josh said he was sitting up and talking after the accident.'

'He was,' Huba said, nodding, 'and he was holding his own all the while he was here.

However, given the distance he fell, we were keeping a close eye on him…'

It wasn't such a quiet day after all, although Marcus was safely out of Theatre by the time Libby's shift ended. She popped up to the unit at the end of the shift to check on him, and was warmed to see his mystery friend sitting with his family in the small waiting room.

'How is he doing?' she asked.

'He's asleep,' his mother said. 'The surgeon said it all went well.'

'I'm so pleased.'

Josh spoke then. 'I'm going to buy him his own control as a get-well gift—no more fighting over it…'

They all laughed.

Libby was indeed pleased that it was a good outcome, and she smiled as she made her weary way to the underground to travel the two stops to her home. Her mind kept drifting to the handsome paramedic who had so clearly insisted that all precautions be taken on scene, and had done what he could to ensure that the gravity of the situation had been quietly stated.

In truth, she would have sent the patient to Resus anyway, until the doctor had carefully assessed him, but his actions had helped articulate the standard procedures, which had made it easier for Libby to stand her ground with Dianne.

Still, all daydreams about a certain gorgeous paramedic faded as she walked through the rain to her small block of flats and down the side entrance.

There to greet her was the biggest fridge ever—right by the stairs up to her apartment. It was thankfully shielded somewhat from the elements, but only because it was half blocking the driveway to the little parking bay behind the flats.

Her fellow residents were having to manoeuvre around it, and they were bemoaning the fact.

Oh, God. Why hadn't she measured it? How had she failed to secure help?

It was just the story of her impulsive life— the very reason that Libby was stuck at five p.m. on a grey winter's night in London, feeling homesick and wondering if she'd made the right move.

Her moving to London hadn't actually been that impulsive. She'd always wanted to work in a major city hospital and well… London!

But the very sociable Libby missed her many friends—especially the ones from the tiny amateur theatre group she'd belonged to. Of course when she had five minutes to breathe

and take stock she'd look to join one here. She
also missed the team at her old A&E department, who had been friendlier than the ones at
The Primary. Her old colleagues had known
that despite her fun, flirty nature there was
a serious head on her shoulders. An anxious
head too. And they had known she took her
work very seriously, but could still manage to
smile and laugh.

Not like the London lot.

Or was it just that there were so many of
them?

Three weeks in and there were still so many
new faces to get used to each and every shift.
Names to remember. Nuances to learn.

Garth, the consultant, was decisive.

Huba was a little hesitant.

May, the Nurse Unit Manager, was all
smiles and friendly comments, but as sharp
as a whip…

Even the London way of speaking was taking a little getting used to.

And then after her shift she would return to
her tiny little flat, and though she had never
minded her own company, it felt very different being alone in London.

Three weeks in, and pretending to love it so
as not to upset her mother was starting to take

its toll. She missed her parents, even if they were a little overbearing.

And now she had her failing ovaries to face. Or not.

She could just put it off, she thought again. Could cancel the appointments and start all over again.

It was a tempting thought.

'Don't be stupid, Libby,' she scolded herself out loud. 'It's time to sort things out.'

She was twenty-eight. Well, twenty-eight and a half. Actually, closer to twenty-nine…

If she put this off, she might well be thirty by the time—

Thirty! Yikes!

Hauling her mind back to the present, Libby attempted to be positive. Brendan was a paramedic and very used to difficult extrications— although it was generally getting patients *down* stairs rather than *up* them.

Why hadn't she thought this through?

Why hadn't she worried adequately?

Libby had acquired the skill from her mother, who worried about everything.

From early morning right through to sleepless night, Helen Bennett worried.

Often with good reason.

Libby's father was a firefighter. All too well Libby could remember creeping down the stairs and seeing her mother's pale face as she anxiously watched the television screen or paced the kitchen.

Sometimes Libby would join her.

Nearly all the time her father would come home unscathed, but there had been more than a few hospital visits to see his colleagues and friends. And, very sadly, she also had the memory of her father getting ready to attend the funeral of a colleague.

Still, Helen Bennett's worrying wasn't just for her husband. It was channelled towards her daughter too.

Growing up, it had been a litany of warnings.

Don't get in a car with someone who's had a drink.

Of course not.

Don't walk home at night alone.

Libby's heels were usually so high she avoided walking as much as she could!

Don't take the night bus.

As a teenager, right up until she was eighteen, her father had always picked her up. She'd left home at eighteen, but even ten years on it would seem Helen would rather her daughter lived at home and was escorted there by two guards after a late shift. Now that she was in London every incident on the news had her mother texting, convinced that Libby must somehow be involved.

Everything in Libby and her father's lives was said and done so as not to upset her mother. Or, rather, everything was secretly done or said so as not to upset her.

Libby was determined not to be like her mother—especially as she had the adventurous spirit of her father. So when her latest relationship had gone south, Libby had decided that so, too, might she.

London.

Only, in this instance she hadn't been cautious enough.

Her innate impulsiveness had won, and now she was living in a flat without a bedroom. As it turned out, the video she'd watched had been of a one-bedroom flat in the same complex, rather than the studio flat she had eventually signed up for. It was her own fault she hadn't read the fine print.

Now, nearly all her stuff remained in storage, as it would have filled the shoebox flat ten times over. Libby had commenced work two days after moving in, and now she had to start looking for somewhere else.

As well as that, her great friend Olivia, who had planned to come and see her, had put off the visit because with hubby and baby there was nowhere for them to stay. Well, even if she'd had a one-bedroom place it would have proved a dreadful squeeze. But Libby wasn't thinking about that now. Even if she hadn't seen as much of Olivia since she'd married, it had been nice knowing she was near…

Her phone bleeped and she pulled it out, hoping it was Brendan to say that he and Rory were on their way.

But instead it was a reminder, asking her to confirm her appointment for an ultrasound.

'What the hell?' A guy in a delivery van who had struggle to manoeuvre around the fridge wound down his window and shouted at her.

'Sorry!' Libby called back.

'Stupid cow!' he yelled, and angrily reversed out.

It was then that all her positivity faded.

His horrible words played on repeat inside her head and it was just the final straw. Libby sat down on the steps, unable to face the fridge, put her head in her hands and for the first time since she'd arrived in London gave in and cried.

Why had she moved here?

It felt like the unfriendliest place in the world.

There was no one she knew to bump into at the shops, as had *always* been the case back home—a dash for bread had often ended up with an hour or so spent in a café, catching up with an old friend, a new friend, a friend of a friend…

Back home she'd have had an army to help her with her fridge…

When she'd moved in to her old flat it had been pizza and wine and fun…

Hearing the roar of a motorcycle, Libby kept her head down, guessing that its rider would no doubt shout at her too.

And, anyway, it felt good to cry.

It felt good, for a moment, to stop being the new one, the happy one, the funny one, the stupid cow—or whatever these people who didn't know her chose to describe her as.

No, she wasn't crying about the fridge. It was about not having any friends in London, and those wretched tests that were looming, and the struggle of being a worrier by nature while also a little wild at heart…

She was mid-sob, and had given up on finding a tissue, when she heard that very nice, very deep voice.

'Is Brendan here?'

She saw black boots, and as her eyes drifted up they clocked an awful lot of black leather.

'Peter!' She stared up at the handsome paramedic and could have kissed him for showing up to help her. But then she realised she'd got his name wrong. 'I mean, Alistair...'

He just stared back at her. On second thoughts, she could happily have kissed him for no reason other than that he was gorgeous! Instead, she sat back on the steps and looked up as he peeled off his black leather gloves and spoke.

'My colleagues call me Perfect Peter behind my back—or to my face to annoy me. It would seem the nursing staff at The Primary do too.'

'No...!' Libby attempted, and then realised there was no getting away from the fact. 'Gosh, I'm so embarrassed.'

'Good,' he said, as if pleased by her mortification.

'It *is* good, actually...' Libby agreed, and watched him frown.

'Why?'

She couldn't bring herself to admit that she'd been pondering on the way home how she was going to have a little fantasy about a hot paramedic called Peter. A hot paramedic called Alistair would be much easier!

'Alistair's a nice name.' Libby settled for that. 'Are you here to help with my fridge?'

'I believe so—unless you've managed to rustle somebody else up?'

'No.'

Gosh, he was seriously good-looking. She had noticed, of course—clearly everybody had, because he wasn't called Perfect Peter for nothing—but now he was dressed in leather and riding a motorbike that would cause her mother to lose her mind if Libby were ever to get on the back of it. So there was a rebellious edge to him too.

'Are we waiting on the steps in the rain?' Alistair asked. 'Or are we going up?'

'We'll go up,' Libby said, delighted by the turn of events and seriously hoping that Brendan would be delayed.

Without thinking, she held out her hand, as a friend might, to be hauled up.

He didn't take it.

And nor should he, of course. They weren't friends or anything.

She wouldn't have held out her hand to the horrible delivery driver had she been here when he'd dropped off the fridge.

It was odd, though, because it felt as if he'd denied her assistance because her gesture had been flirtatious, although he was probably just annoyed at having to lug her fridge. Especially as he had his physical assessment tomorrow.

He'd pass. Libby was rather sure of that from looking at him!

But they wouldn't be waiting in Libby's little flat, because as they started to go in a car squeezed up the drive and Brendan waved.

'Here he is,' Alistair said, as Brendan got out of the car and huffed his way towards them. Then he added rather drily. 'My lifting companion.'

'Is it an important assessment tomorrow?' Libby asked.

'Very.'

'Look, I don't want you getting injured. I'm sure that Brendan and I, between us—'

He cut her off with a look. Not a macho chauvinist look, just a blunt look that told her what she already knew: there was not a chance in hell of her and Brendan moving it.

'Thanks so much for this,' she said, both to him and to Brendan. 'I really do appreciate it...'

'Which one's yours?' Alistair asked, looking up at the flats.

'Two hundred and one,' Libby said.

'Second floor?'

'Yes.'

He proceeded to go up the first flight of steps, to see what they were up against, and then drew a finger picture of the layout for Brendan.

'Can't we just get on with it?' called Brendan.

'You don't learn safety by accident,' Alistair

called back, quoting an old saying, and Libby wanted to giggle as Brendan muttered and rolled his eyes.

Alistair certainly planned his lifts!

Brendan was to go first, while Alistair got the heavy end. Libby stood by as they lifted, feeling useless. All she could do was grab the electrical cord when it slipped and trailed on the ground.

'Leave that, please,' Alistair said.

'It might cause an accident,' she pointed out.

'Leave it,' he said through gritted teeth as he took the full weight of the fridge.

''I'm just trying to help…'

'If you want to help, then go up and open the doors,' Alistair replied.

Libby climbed the stairs to her flat and propped open all the doors, then quickly threw a few cups in the sink and kicked a bra behind the sofa-bed. Glancing across the room, she looked at the gap in her doll's-house-sized kitchen units and lost all hope that the fridge was going to fit there.

She could hear them coming up the stairs—Brendan's heavy breathing and Alistair's clear instructions. She hovered at the door, rather like a family member might linger in the corridor when there was a sick relative in Resus.

'Right,' Alistair said, and then, 'The flat's just to the left…'

She stepped back from the doorway, and it was Brendan who gave instructions now. 'Down in three, two, one—now.'

Brendan was red-faced and sweaty. God, she hoped he didn't have a heart attack or something dreadful.

After a brief respite, they rocked the heavy fridge the remaining short distance into her flat.

'Where's the kitchen?' Alistair asked.

'Just here is fine,' Libby said, and Brendan gratefully straightened up then arched his back. 'Completely fine! I can slide it from here. You guys have done more than enough. I mean, honestly, I can manage from here…'

Brendan seemed relieved, but Alistair looked at her suspiciously. 'I'll push it through.'

'No need,' Libby said, and found that she was blushing as if she herself had been heaving the fridge up the stairs.

'You haven't measured it, have you?' Alistair accused. 'That's why earlier today, at work, you were standing with your hand on top of your head in the kitchen…'

She should be flattered that he'd noticed, let alone recalled what she'd been doing, but instead she was embarrassed as he brushed past her into her tiny, tiny kitchen as Brendan leaned against the wall and got his breath back.

'It will fit,' Alistair said, reluctantly hissing between clenched teeth.

'I don't think so...' Libby gulped.

'So you let us drag it up here, thinking it wouldn't fit?'

'I need a fridge,' Libby said, shrugging. 'It might have had to live in here for a little while.'

She saw his eyes take in the studio flat and the sofa-bed she had not folded back this morning.

She was burning red as he pushed and rocked the fridge over to the units, then left it standing in the middle of the kitchen.

'It doesn't fit, does it?' Libby checked.

'It will, but you have to let it stand for three hours,' he said.

'Oh, no.' Brendan shook his head. 'It's been upright since it's been dropped off, so it should be fine.'

'It wasn't very upright on the stairs,' Alistair said, turning those heavenly chocolate eyes to Libby. 'Keep it unplugged for three hours or you risk damaging the compressor.'

'Sure...'

'*Then* you can slide it in.'

'I shall. Look, thank you, guys. I'd offer you a cuppa, but I don't have any milk...' She glanced at her new fridge as if in explanation. 'Or a beer. But...'

'Have you got any glasses?' Brendan asked.

Actually, she didn't.

All her glasses were in storage, with the rest of her stuff. She'd been planning to buy a few cheap ones to see her through on her next day off.

Libby did have four mugs—all of which were now sitting in the sink. She rushed over to wash them, before handing a clean one filled with cold water to Brendan.

'Alistair?'

'No, thank you.'

'I've got chocolate biscuits,' she said, but they both declined. Clearly they were more than ready to go home.

'Seriously,' Alistair said as he left, 'wait three hours.'

'I shall. Look, thank you. It really was kind. Thank you, Brendan. And Alistair, I hope your physical goes well tomorrow.'

He simply nodded, and then was gone.

She breathed a sigh of relief as she closed the door behind them. No one that sexy had ever been in her little doll's house studio flat before.

Actually, no one that sexy had been so close to her bed before!

She looked at her fridge with delight, and

gave it a little pat. She thought about Alistair's sternly delivered wise words about waiting three hours. But surely she should check that it worked? Just briefly…?

Impulsiveness won out and Libby plugged it in.

Light.

Yay!

Forgetting all Alistair's warnings, she pushed the fridge back and was delighted to find that it fitted.

Just.

Certainly she wouldn't be able to put a broom or a mop by the side of it—or anything, really. But she had a fridge, and she could now have real meals. In fact, she would go shopping right away…

Picking up her bag, and still in her coat, she opened the door to find—

'Alistair!'

'I dropped a glove…'

'Oh.' She cast her eyes around the bedroom/ lounge and realised it must be in the kitchen. 'I'll go and have a look.' She gave him a lovely smile. 'Wait there.'

But he did not wait there…

It might have been disconcerting to have a man ignore her request to wait at the door, but they both knew exactly why he brushed past her and in two long strides reached her kitchen.

'Good God!' he said, when he saw how quickly she'd dismissed his instructions.

He yanked the fridge out, turned it off, and gave her a long and tedious lecture about oil and compressors…or something like that…

Yet he made 'tedious' sexy! She could have gazed into those velvet eyes for ever, whatever the subject matter.

'Have you no patience?' he demanded finally.

'None,' Libby admitted happily.

Absolutely none. Because though she had known him for just a few minutes, and had only met him for the first time earlier that day, she was suddenly frantic for his kiss.

'I often tend to regret my impulsive decisions…'

Libby's voice trailed off as she realised she was warning herself that chasing after a kiss from this gorgeous man was foolhardy at best.

After all, she barely knew his name.

'Regret?' he asked, with that lovely full mouth, and she saw his jaw was a touch darker than it had been this morning.

'When I don't think things through.'

He opened his mouth, as if to say something,

and then he chose not to. Bizarrely, she wondered if he might be thinking about kissing too.

Libby didn't usually have such random kissing thoughts.

Clearly nor did he usually have the kind of thoughts he seemed to be having, because he suddenly seemed a bit shocked. He looked away and took a step to the side and swiped his glove from the floor.

'Come on,' he said, and took her arm.

'Where are we going?'

'For a drink and dinner. We're going to wait out those three hours together. Have you got your keys?'

'Yes, I was about to go to the shops.'

They headed down the steps and Libby took out her phone.

'Where should we go? There's a pub near the Tube station that looks like it does decent food…'

'Okay.'

'I'll meet you there.'

'I can give you a ride.'

'Oh, no. I'm not getting on your bike.' She shook her head.

It wasn't her mother's dire warnings that held her back. A stint on Orthopaedics and her time working in Emergency had put Libby off motorbikes for good. However, she did really, really want a drink and dinner.

'I'll meet you there.'

'Why? I've got a spare helmet.'

'I have a very strict rule,' Libby said, smiling. 'I don't go on motorbikes. Or anything with two wheels, come to think of it...'

She thought it was probably still cold and wet outside, and since it was too far to walk and not look like a drowned rat, she said, 'I'll get a cab.'

'Sure,' he replied. 'No cheating, though.'

'Cheating?'

'Dashing back in...' He glanced to her flat.

'I don't cheat,' Libby said, thinking he really seemed to know her far too well.

Because she'd have loved to dash back in, tidy up a little—herself, rather than the flat— and not look quite so bedraggled for her evening with the sexiest, most perfect paramedic.

'Look, I'm calling for a cab now.'

Annoyingly, he waited till her car arrived, and ten minutes later they were outside what appeared from the outside to be a very nice pub. Only, on entering it, they discovered it turned out to be one of those family ones, full of boisterous children and frazzled parents.

'It's noisy,' Libby said, a bit taken back by all the people. 'Should we have booked?'

But it would seem there was space for them after all.

They were led to a high table with bar stools, where they disrobed and de-leathered. Libby perched on her stool and tried to look at the menu rather than at his lovely forearms.

He wore a grey jumper, and he had gorgeous black hair on his arms and a jut of black chest hair at the base of his neck.

And he'd caught her looking.

She flushed and fought for something to say. 'I'm getting this,' Libby said. 'I mean it.' She would have no arguments. 'I was going to get you some wine or whatever, for moving my fridge, so this makes it easier.'

'Fine.'

Not even a smidge of protest!

He decided to have steak with pepper sauce, potato wedges, no salad and water, while Libby was tempted by the scampi, because she hadn't had it in for ever. But she didn't want to smell of fish. Not that they were going to be kissing, but she couldn't help considering these things, because she considered everything—and hadn't they shared a charged moment back in her flat, when he had confronted her about the fridge? Could kissing be on the cards after all?

She was being ridiculous.

Libby decided she would also have steak, but with salad. And, because she wasn't going home on a motorbike and she was exhausted from worrying about her fridge, a glass of wine.

She returned from the bar with their drinks and two tokens. 'We get a free trip to the dessert station!'

'Cheers,' Alistair said, and they chinked glasses. 'Here's to your fridge.'

'It's been awful not having one.'

'It really wasn't worth crying over.'

'It might have been when my neighbours found out it was *my* fridge blocking the drive.'

'True... How long have you worked at The Primary?' he asked.

'Three weeks.' Libby sighed. 'And I still feel like it's my first day. I worked in Norfolk before, in a tiny hospital compared to The Primary. I can't believe how busy it is...how much of an area it covers.'

'And it's getting bigger...' he agreed.

Their meal arrived and Libby was glad she hadn't ordered the scampi, as the steak looked delicious.

'I'm starving,' Alistair said. 'So how come you moved from Norfolk?'

'I just...' Libby thought for a moment. 'I was very happy there, but I wanted to know what it was like to work in a big trauma centre, and I really wanted a couple of years in London. So…'

'You like Emergency?'

'Reluctantly.' Libby nodded.

'Reluctantly?' He frowned.

'Well, it's very…' How best to say it? 'I adore it, but I can't stand it at the same time…'

He frowned again.

'I worry about everything.'

'Except fridge compressors,' he pointed out, and Libby laughed.

'As I said, when I don't worry enough—or when I worry about the wrong things—I tend to regret it…' She looked right at him. 'I got caught, didn't I.'

'You did.'

Only, she wasn't regretting it now!

And, from the way he held her eyes for easily seventeen seconds, neither was he.

Eighteen seconds.

Nineteen…

She dragged her eyes from his beckoning gaze and tried to get back to the question and best explain how the daily witnessing of the fragility of life affected her.

'Take our friend today, who had the gaming controller accident.'

'The long fall?' he checked.

'Yes. It's put me off standing on a bed for life...'

'Do you regularly stand on the bed?'

'Yes.' Libby nodded and he smiled, but then she asked a more serious question. 'Does it trouble you? I mean, you must see far worse than I do.'

After all, he would see the patients who didn't even make it to the hospital, and he would see seriously injured people outside of the relatively controlled and resourced environment of A&E.

'Most of the time it's a lot like social work,' he said.

'Not all of the time?'

'No...' He was clearly thinking about her question as to whether the sights he saw troubled him. 'I guess it makes me appreciate life—and it's perhaps taught me not to take unnecessary risks...'

'Yet you ride a motorbike?'

'Well, I was once thinking of being a rapid responder,' Alistair said.

And thankfully he was looking down, slicing the last of his steak, so missed her little shudder.

Libby actually grimaced as she made a mental note never to fall for someone who zipped around on a motorbike for a living.

He looked up. 'What do you think of London?'

'I'm sure I'll love it,' Libby said, 'when I get a chance to see it. My first round of days off was spent arguing with my estate agent.'

'About…?'

'I thought I was getting a one-bedroom flat. I signed the lease without viewing it…'

He stared, but thankfully didn't tell her how stupid that had been.

'How long's the lease?' he asked.

'Three months,' Libby said.

'Well, at least you got that part right.'

'All my things are in storage—as I soon as I saw the place I knew there was no way they'd fit. I do actually have glasses and a fridge of my own…even a bed…' She let out a glum sigh. 'I've had to put a hold on the delivery and just buy a sofa-bed and a few cups and a kettle and such while I work out what to do…'

'And a fridge?'

Libby nodded. 'I'll probably sell it to who-ever leases the flat after me. Although…' She rolled her eyes heavenwards.

'Go on.'

'As much as the agent may have exaggerated the size of my dwelling, the price is on a par with the area and I *really* like it… I'm trying to decide if I can survive in a shoebox just to be close to the underground, the parks…' She smiled. 'It's a lot greener than I dared hope. Do you live close by?'

'A few miles,' he said. 'Regent's Canal—just a short walk away. Do you miss home?'

'There hasn't been time, and I'm in touch a lot.'

'How old are you?'

'Twenty-eight,' Libby said. 'Well, twenty-eight and a half…'

He smiled.

He was just so easy to talk to…

They clicked—or at least it felt like that to Libby as she told him about her friend Olivia and her husband and baby.

'I was telling her about this gorgeous bar, how incredible it sounded, and she said that when she came to visit she really wanted to try it. And do you know what happened?'

'Yes,' Alistair said.

'You don't.'

'I do,' he said, mopping up the last smear of pepper sauce with his steak. 'She asked if you'd babysit.'

Libby's mouth fell open. 'How did you know?'

'Because I work with a lot of parents of young children and they're always on the scrounge for babysitters.'

'Do they ask you?' she smiled.

'No, because when I congratulate them on

their happy news I make a point of telling them upfront that I won't be babysitting.' He topped up his water. 'Not even if I'm a godparent.'

'Oh.' Libby looked across the table to him. 'And are you a godparent?'

'Twice. Each year I take them to see a pantomime and the Christmas lights…'

'Pantomime!' Libby was delighted, and told him about the tiny little amateur theatre group she had been so heavily involved in. 'I have to find one here. I mean, there are loads, but…' She sighed. 'I'll be a very small fish.'

'Were you a big fish at home?' Alistair asked.

'I played the narrator in *Joseph*,' she told him proudly. 'Admittedly, it was a very small production…' She waved at him to go on. 'Your godchildren?'

'Well, I also try to do a daytrip in the Easter school holidays, and one in the summer—even if it's just a visit to the ambulance station…'

'They must love it.'

'Oh, yes. So their parents know better than to jeopardise that by asking me to give up a Saturday night so they can go to a wine bar.'

'I tend to get caught on the hop.'

'Well, be careful,' he warned, 'or you'll have your friend, husband and baby all crammed into your flat and you looking after the baby while they go to the bar…'

He must have seen her pressed lips.

'Do *not* get a bigger place,' he warned.

He was the first person to make her feel better about having the tiniest flat in the world.

'If they want to come and see you then they can book a hotel—or tell them you'll catch them the next time you're home.'

'I like your way of thinking.'

'And find the name of a good babysitting service should they actually come and see you.'

'They'll never come!' Libby laughed, and then her laughter faded because she knew it was kind of true...

Not so much the babysitting part—she loved babies—but she did feel a little adrift from her friends who had settled down...

Alistair made being single sound like an attribute—something to relish. Gosh, he made saying no to friends with children sound possible...doable. He was just so...in tune with his own priorities. He did not sway to please, and she liked that.

Really, really liked that.

'So, you have a physical assessment tomorrow?' said Libby. 'Is that a work thing?'

Alistair nodded.

In fact he was near the end of a long application process to get into the Hazardous Area

Response Team, and was eventually aiming to work for the Paramedic Tactical Response Unit.

In truth, he rather doubted he would get accepted into HART. Not because of the physical assessment or the studying or anything like that. It was the team player part.

He was very independent, and although he liked being in a team at times, he liked taking charge and working alone too. The HART application process was thorough, and there was no showing only your best side to advantage.

All sides were being scrutinised.

So he wasn't letting anyone in on his plans. Well, a couple of colleagues knew, like Brendan and Lina, but aside from that he was trying to keep it under wraps. He didn't want to discuss it now, with Libby, so he left his response at a nod and moved on.

'Do you want dessert?' he asked.

'Always.' Libby smiled and pushed a token towards him. It was then that their fingers brushed—or rather, their fingers met.

It felt electric.

But also more than electric. Because when you come into contact with electricity, the natural response was to pull back.

Neither of them did, so Libby amended her

thought inside her head. It felt *magnetic*, because now his fingers were toying with the tips of hers.

And he didn't let go. In fact, he turned her hand over and commented on the smooth pale skin.

'For someone who must use alcohol rub a thousand times a day, you have very soft hands.'

'Because I use hand cream a thousand and one times a day,' Libby said, smiling. 'Well, that's possibly an exaggeration...'

She examined his very neat nails and rather lovely long fingers and thought how nice they felt, lingering in her own.

'Yours are soft too.' She looked up to his smile and met his eyes. 'Do you use hand cream?'

'Much to Brendan's mirth, I do.' He nodded.

For the first time in memory, Libby found she actually didn't want dessert. Instead, she wanted to sit playing with his fingers and marvelling at the feel of his skin against hers.

'I'm so pleased you dropped your glove and had to come back.'

'I didn't drop it,' Alistair said, and she looked up from their joined fingers to chocolate-brown eyes that knew how to flirt. 'At least, not by accident.'

'Oh!'

She loved it that he didn't hide it—that he didn't pretend this night was an accident. She loved it that he had, in fact, engineered it. Thinking about that made a smile spread across her face. A smile watched by those gorgeous dark eyes.

Suddenly, that feeling she'd had beside the fridge was back...that feeling that she was possibly about to be kissed!

'Dessert?' Alistair said, separating their hands as a rather grumpy waitress came to clear their plates.

Gosh, she thought as she helped herself to ice-cream at the dessert bar, never in a million years could she have imagined that her difficult day would turn out to be so promising.

So very promising.

He made the rather noisy surroundings melt away into nothing, so she could imagine they were the only two people in the world. Alistair made a pub dinner exciting.

Special.

It was as if Libby had chosen the most romantic restaurant in existence.

Still, even with dessert they couldn't stay at the table for three hours when the pub was this busy. They got up to leave, but both were happy not to part ways as they stepped out into the night.

In fact, with no plates or grumpy waitresses hurrying them on, they freely held hands. As naturally as if they'd been together a hundred years and held hands every day.

Libby went into the off-licence next door and bought Brendan a nice bottle of wine in a bag with a bow as his reward for helping with the fridge. Since she'd bought dinner for Alistair, they were even now.

Then they walked to a small corner shop, and Libby bought a couple of essentials for her new fridge—milk, butter, cheese…

'It'll be nice to have milk in my coffee in the morning,' Libby said, and then pressed her lips together, because everything she said sounded as if she was flirting.

He didn't answer that.

She selected two chocolate treats at the checkout.

Well, she selected one easily and then dithered over her second choice, her hand hesitating between a bar of hazelnut chocolate and one of chocolate-covered nougat.

'Sorry,' she said, glancing up to the shopkeeper, who she caught smothering a smile, and then looking to Alistair, who stood patiently behind her. 'This one,' she said, choosing the nougat, instantly regretting it, but trying not to show it.

She paid for her purchases and then Alistair bought a fondant-filled chocolate egg. 'I'll have it when I get home.'

Libby pouted as they walked out the store. 'Now *I* want a chocolate egg.'

He didn't answer—just looked up at the sky, which had turned to black as large drops of rain started to splash down.

'I've got my umbrella,' Libby said, opening up her vast bag. 'I think…'

She didn't have her umbrella.

'I must have left it at home,' she said, rummaging in it even as he steered them into a covered doorway. 'Typical. The one time…'

She looked up, and suddenly umbrellas really didn't matter because he was pulling her close.

'Are we going to wait it out here?' Libby asked.

'It's been almost three hours since we left the fridge,' he said. 'Aside from that, I don't think the rain's going anywhere.' As she reached for her phone, to summon a cab, his hand gently caught her fingers to stop her calling. 'I said it's been *almost* three hours. Can't risk you turning that fridge on…'

'Oh…' She happily put her phone back in her bag. 'Well, it's true that I don't have any patience.'

'Exactly,' he agreed, and pulled her into him.

She gave in then. She had waited three hours, after all, and when it came to it she found she had never known a kiss like it.

God, he was so sexy—because there wasn't any awkwardness. It was just a thorough rainy night kiss.

She was suddenly mindful that at any moment the little handles on Brendan's wine bag might break, so they stopped kissing for a second so she could put it carefully into her shoulder bag, and then got back to their deep kiss.

His lips were divine—firm and incredibly thorough—and he held her so firmly she didn't even have to lean on the wall for support.

He even took care of the carrier bag with her fridge food in it, grabbing it and lowering it to the floor.

'Luckily no glass in that one,' she said, and then his hands slid inside her coat and they got back to kissing again. She had never—not once in her life—wanted someone so badly, so urgently. It felt as if she'd been wanting him since this morning—and she undoubtedly had.

She was pressed against him, and it was very

clear he wanted her too. But just when she was going to suggest they make a run for the flat—because it felt imperative that they must not part—it was he who pulled her hips and his mouth back.

'We're going to stop,' Alistair said. 'Because I have to strip off tomorrow during my assessment and I don't think we're going to be gentle, do you?'

Libby gulped, because usually she was so boring at sex. She didn't think it was anything special, if past experience was anything to go by. But she wanted to pinch him, and taste him, and just…

He brought out something in her that no one ever had before.

'I think you're being very sensible,' she said.

'Sometimes,' Alistair said, caressing her hips and looking at her with a hunger that had nothing to do with food, 'I wish I wasn't so sensible…'

'So do I,' Libby agreed. 'But you're completely right.' She was practically hanging off his neck. 'Thank you for all your help today. When did you change your mind about coming to help with the fridge?'

'I'm not telling you,' he said, kissing her neck and cupping her breast through her jumper.

She leant against him and realised that she

had never been so consumed by desire for someone. So instantly attracted to another person. And the best part was that it was clearly entirely reciprocated.

'Please tell me...' she whispered. 'When did you change your mind?'

'I was always going to come.'

'Were you?' She smiled and could feel the pressure of his hands as he resisted pulling her back in.

'Call for your cab...' he said, and she reluctantly did so.

Unfortunately, her car was all of two minutes away, which left time for just one more kiss before her phone bleeped again. 'It's approaching... Damn!'

He laughed at her angry hiss. 'Thank you for dinner.'

'You're very welcome.' She looked at the torrential rain. 'How will you get home?'

'I'm used to it,' he said, zipping up his jacket.

She stared out onto the street and watched a zillion headlights glaring, then a silver car pulled up. 'I'm going to go and plug in my fridge now.'

'Hold on.' He halted her, pulling her back into the doorway. He took her phone and checked the registration of the arriving car against the one she had ordered. 'Yes, it's good. Always check!'

'Okay!'

'I mean it. Don't just jump into some random car...'

'Yes, Alistair.'

'And remember—next time you buy a fridge, or whatever, measure twice, cut once...'

Libby laughed and made a dash for it in the pelting rain.

As she sat in the car for the short drive home she felt an unexpected bulge in her pocket. She reached her hand in and found a shiny foil-wrapped fondant-filled egg...and let out a happy sigh of surprise.

She was still wearing a smile as she let herself into her teeny-tiny flat. She immediately plugged in the fridge and turned on the switch, admiring her own restraint as she waited before opening the door.

'Let there be light!' Libby said.

And there was.

And also, suddenly, a booming clap of thunder.

More sheets of rain had started to fall, and if she'd had Alistair's number she'd have texted him to make sure he'd got home okay—and not just because she was a worrier.

It was filthy weather out there.

And while eating her lovely chocolate egg, she peered out at the storm-laden night and worried about him on his motorbike.

Worried a lot.

CHAPTER TWO

ALISTAIR HAD MADE it safely home.

Well, Libby assumed that to be the case, because all the paramedics the next day seemed to be in a good mood, and pleasant, so presumably he hadn't died.

Libby was seesawing between feeling dreadfully loose, because of the nature of that kiss, while simultaneously trying to reel herself in and dismiss it as just a kiss—because of course he would have kissed many women...

But the memory of it was perfect.

So perfect that she almost didn't want to take her upcoming days off, because it meant there would be no chance of seeing him.

In truth, she had no idea about the paramedics' shift rotas and days on and off or such things. She tried to ask Rory, who was back from his sick leave, but he seemed to infer that she was angling to go out with him and said, 'I finish around seven, if you want to catch up?'

'No, no!' Libby quickly declined—perhaps a little too emphatically. And then wished she had been more polite. 'I've got so much to do… with the move and everything.'

Phew.

Still, from what she *had* managed to gather from Rory, paramedics worked four long shifts, a mixture of days and nights, and swapped partners a lot—not in the swinging sense, of course.

By her next shift she'd worked out that Alistair was presumably now on nights, and the thought that she wouldn't see him had her sagging a little as she checked the equipment in Resus.

'Did you ever get your fridge sorted?' asked May.

'I did,' Libby said, nodding. 'Brendan and Alistair helped.'

'That's nice.'

'Yes,' Libby said. 'At first I didn't think they'd help…'

'Oh, Brendan's like that.'

While Brendan was indeed nice, she had been trying to steer the conversation onto Alistair, but no matter how much Libby tried she could not glean a thing from any of her colleagues.

And there were so many things she wanted to glean!

'Speak of the devil,' May said, and Libby started when she saw Brendan and Alistair wheeling in a patient who was hidden under a silver foil blanket. 'Shouldn't you be at home?' May asked the two unshaven paramedics, who looked more than a little bleary-eyed.

They must be at the tail-end of their night shift, Libby thought.

'We've been on scene for a while,' Alistair explained, 'and now we're well into overtime. This is Mrs Anna Dalton,' he went on. 'Eighty-seven years old, suspected fracture neck of the femur. She had a fall on her way to bed around eleven last night and has been on the floor ever since. Her daughter was unable to get her up and called for help at five a.m.'

That was a long time to wait before asking for help, Libby thought, briefly meeting Alistair's eyes. She guessed she might get a more detailed handover away from the bedside.

'It was a difficult extraction,' Alistair said, and then directed his next words to his patient. 'I'm just telling the nurse we had some trouble getting you out to the ambulance.'

Libby knew there must be more to it, because Mrs Dalton was like a tiny bird and they would have had little trouble moving her, but the reason for their difficulties would have to wait for now.

'Hello, Mrs Dalton.' Libby pulled back the foil blanket and looked at the frail lady as Alistair listed the drugs that had been given on scene, then reported that she was hypothermic and had a past history of mild dementia.

Her temperature was worryingly low, so Libby took her through to Resus, where they could keep a much closer eye on her. 'Where's her daughter?'

'She wanted to stay at home,' Alistair said. 'The daughter's name is Rosemary.'

Mrs Dalton spoke for the first time. 'Where's my Rosemary?'

'Rosemary's at home, Mrs Dalton,' Alistair said, then added to Libby, 'Rosemary has MS and isn't very mobile, but I said someone would call and update her.'

'Of course.'

When Libby had got Mrs Dalton on to a Resus bed, May came over and started setting up the warming blanket as Huba examined the diminutive lady and Alistair went through the handover again. Then he nodded his head at Libby, and then towards the door, to indicate he wanted to talk. Even though he was pulling her away, she knew there would be no flirting at work with Alistair—no departure from perfect protocol and procedure.

'The set-up at home isn't good,' he told her. 'There's a hoarding issue—just stuff *everywhere*. We could barely get through to the lounge. Mrs Dalton gets upset if it's mentioned. Rosemary's doing her best, but she's barely able to take care of herself, let alone her mother. From what I can make out they really don't have any support.'

'None?' Libby frowned.

'The place is unkempt and freezing. There were a few cans of soup in the kitchen, but apart from that there was nothing I could see. Just tea and long-life milk. And Rosemary didn't want to come in with her mother. She said she was worried about how she'd get home, but I don't think she's actually been out of the house in a very long time. I've called their GP and asked him to do a home visit.'

Libby recalled what Alistair had said about a lot of his job being social work.

'The home situation really isn't safe,' he finished.

'Okay.'

The daughter wasn't their patient, and didn't want help, but it was clear the paramedics had been concerned enough to have requested that the GP intervene.

'I'll call her myself,' Libby said. 'What's her surname?'

'The same—Dalton.'

As May fussed over Mrs Dalton, Libby managed to duck out to the changing rooms and to her locker. Catching the paramedics as they left, she gave Brendan his bottle of wine in the gift bag with the bow on it.

'Thank you so much for moving my fridge,' she said.

'That's great, Libby, thank you,' Brendan said, and then held it out to Alistair. 'I should give this to you, seeing how last-minute it was...'

'Brendan, it's for you,' Libby said, frowning. And then it dawned on her that Brendan thought she'd bought one bottle of wine between them. 'I've got one for...' She stopped and glanced at Alistair. 'Well, I...'

She was stuck, because they all knew he'd been at his physical yesterday, so she couldn't say she'd already given him one, and she didn't want to admit they'd been out to dinner.

'I thought Alistair was off today.' She risked a glance at Alistair's impassive features and could see the twinkle in his eyes that told her he was laughing inside at her little dilemma. 'I'll bring yours in, Alistair, and keep it in my locker for next time I see you.'

'Thanks!' Alistair said carefully. 'That's very thoughtful of you.'

'Thanks very much,' Brendan said as the duo headed off. 'Alison will be thrilled.'

Libby guessed Alison must be his wife. 'Have a good sleep!' she called to them both, although her words were really aimed at Alistair.

So now she'd have to buy another bottle of wine, when she was as broke as a church mouse after the move, the new sofa-bed and fridge, and having to pay for the storage of her own furniture. And then there was that dinner… There had been no manly protest that he would pay instead.

Ha-ha!

She liked him far too much. Not that she had time to think about dark-haired sexy paramedics, because the day was shaping up to be a busy one.

A lot of Libby's morning was taken up with Mrs Dalton, and also speaking with her daughter over the telephone.

'What's happening with Mum?' That was naturally the main question she had.

'She's doing better,' Libby said, knowing Mrs Dalton was back from X-Ray. 'Thankfully her hip isn't broken, but there is an old fracture there.'

'That was ages ago.'

'How does she usually get around?'

'We manage.'

Alistair had been right. From all Libby could make out Rosemary had been struggling to take care of her mother, especially as her own health had declined. She was too scared to go out in case she caught anything and brought it back to her mother, and too nervous to let anyone into their home because of her mother's accumulation of stuff. On top of that, she was worried about putting the heating on, and had a nasty cough herself.

'Have you heard from your GP?' Libby asked.

'He called, but I told him I'm fine. I only called the ambulance because I couldn't get Mum up by myself.'

Gosh, she was stubborn. And she really didn't want anyone coming into her home.

'How do you manage for shopping?' Libby tried to get more details.

'My brother takes care of it.'

'How often is that?'

'When he can.'

In the end, it all took more than a morning.

Eventually a social worker came down and called the GP surgery himself. Fortunately Alistair's referral had been comprehensive enough that they had planned a home visit despite Rosemary's assurances that all was fine.

Mrs Dalton was still awaiting a bed on the geriatric ward by the time the end of Libby's shift rolled around. Libby was just helping her to open some sandwiches and add sugar to her tea when May came in and smiled at their patient.

'How are you doing, Mrs Dalton?'

She was more interested in the sandwiches than answering, and Libby explained that the wait for a bed on the ward was going to be another hour. 'I promised Mrs Dalton's daughter I'd call her when she was moved.'

'I've just come off the phone with her GP,' May said. 'He's done a home visit and Rosemary is going to be admitted to a medical ward.'

'Oh!' Libby was relieved to hear it. From her own conversations with Rosemary it had been clear that there was a lot going on, but her reluctance to go out or let anyone in to her home meant nothing had been addressed.

'She's coming via Emergency for a chest X-ray.'

May gave Libby a wink. Usually a direct admission went straight to the ward, but this way perhaps Rosemary would be able to manage a brief visit with her mother.

May smiled over to the patient. 'You're getting a visitor soon, Mrs Dalton.'

Mrs Dalton just peeled open her sandwich and peered inside before nibbling on it. She looked so much better than she had this morning. Her cheeks were pink and she'd chatted a little with Libby. She'd even walked to the toilet, but she had required considerable help.

'Go home,' May said to Libby, and Libby nodded.

After wishing Mrs Dalton goodnight, she headed out, walking with May to the changing rooms.

'I don't know how they've managed for so long,' she said.

'Barely,' May said. 'The GP said she was very reluctant to let him in. Apparently there's a hoarding problem at the house.'

'The paramedics said the same.' Libby told her. 'Hopefully now they'll get the help they need.'

'Let's hope,' May agreed. 'You're on days off now?'

Libby nodded again and wished May a good evening, before gathering her things and going home.

She was so tired that she almost dozed on the Tube, and she wondered if she might just sleep her way through every stop until the end of the line. But she jolted awake just in time, and gradually made her rather listless way home, where she had a shower and then wrapped herself up in her dressing gown and flopped onto the sofa, almost too tired to open it up and make the bed.

Why hadn't she gone shopping on the way home from work? she scolded herself. Now she was clean and cosy she didn't want to get dressed and go back out.

Tomorrow she would do a massive shop and get organised. Four days off in a row meant she could finally get on top of things. But that didn't help her grumbling stomach tonight!

You are not getting food delivered, Libby told herself.

There had been far too much of that since she'd arrived in the city. As well as moving, finding out her flat was missing a bedroom, putting a hold on her furniture delivery and sorting out storage, she had also started a new job, so there had barely been time to breathe, let alone shop for healthy, balanced meals.

She really ought to get up, get dressed and go out in search of something better than delivery food.

But then she'd have to cook it as well.

Bleh...

Suddenly then she heard—or rather *felt*—the

throbbing purr of an engine in the driveway
beneath her window. It sounded like a motorbike... *His* motorbike, maybe?

Libby found she was holding her breath.

It wasn't.

It couldn't be.

Yet she lay on her sofa-bed, resisting peeking
and desperately trying not to get her hopes up.

If she looked out of the window then it
wouldn't be him.

If she got up and ran a comb through her
hair, quickly slicked on some mascara and
pulled on something more attractive than her
ancient robe, it wouldn't be him.

Of course it isn't him, she told her rapidly
beating heart.

Yet as she lay there, ears on elastic, biting her
bottom lip as she heard footsteps on the stairs
outside, Libby found herself relishing the an-
ticipation.

There was a smile spreading across her face
as she listened to the sound of heavy footsteps
getting nearer and nearer. There was a pause,
and then a firm knock on her door, and hope
shot like a flare into the night sky.

Oh, why hadn't she put on mascara or
changed...?

Because it was probably a delivery for another flat in the building, Libby reminded her-

self as she jumped from the couch and walked to her door.

She opened it, bracing for disappointment while still hoping all the same. There were plenty of other residents who might have decided to order food in rather than go out into the cold winter's night.

Hope won!

'Alistair!' She grinned like an idiot. 'Did you drop another glove?'

'No,' he said. 'And, just so you know, I deliberately dropped it before, so I could come back.'

'Oh!' Libby's heart turned over in her chest.

She loved it that he didn't lie or play games... that he admitted his attraction up front.

It thrilled her.

As well as that, he had the unfair advantage of having spent the day in bed, and he was looking all refreshed and lethal to her senses in his leather biker gear.

And, even better, he came bearing gifts!

He handed her a tall paper bag with a red foil rosette attached to the top. Peeking in, she could see it was a bottle of wine.

'That's for you to give to me at work,' he said. 'Put it in your bag now, so you don't forget.'

'Thank you!'

'And this is for both of us for now.'

He held up a white carry-out bag, from which she caught delectable wafts of curry and spice. From under his arm peeked a bottle of icy bubbly wine.

'Just what I wanted!'

She had to fight not to leap forward and kiss him, and instead stepped back to let him in. *Play it cool, Libby*, she warned herself.

'You've rescued me from going shopping.'

'In your dressing gown?' he enquired.

'I was about to get dressed and...' She gave in. 'You're right. I was never going to go shopping tonight, but I was trying not to get food delivered—again.'

'Why not? You've been working all week,' he pointed out as he put all the goodies onto her kitchen bench. 'Anyway, it's cold out there.'

It was exceedingly warm in here...

Well, not technically, since the heater didn't spread its warmth very far. It was more that she was burning up inside.

He unzipped his jacket to reveal a thin black jumper beneath. He looked around for somewhere to put the jacket.

'There's a hanger on the back of my front door.'

'Thanks.'

He went to hang up his jacket and she heard

the sound of his boots being unzipped. It made her feel fluttery and perturbed—but in a good way—and she looked up quickly as he returned.

Gosh, he was very big for her little kitchen, and she'd realised the grumble in her stomach had nothing to do with the cartons he was pulling out of the take-out bag.

'How was your physical?' Libby asked as she took out two plates and put them on the bench.

'I'm a fine specimen, apparently.'

'They didn't say that…' Libby grinned.

'They might have,' Alistair replied. 'It was very thorough.'

She bit down on her lip, resisting asking, *How thorough?*

Resisting provoking him.

Except, when it came to Alistair, she simply could not resist.

She peeled open a corner of one of the lids, even though she didn't really want to—because how could she possibly be thinking of food with Alistair standing behind her? She wanted to turn to him, or at least turn her head, and she felt her breath hitch.

She didn't want to resist.

'How thorough?' Libby asked, in a voice that was a little bit croaky.

'Oh, you know…' Alistair said. 'They checked my back…'

'Really?' she squeaked, as he ran a finger down the length of her spine and the light touch almost shot her into orbit.

'My neck…' he added, as he lifted her hair and breathed on her neck, and then gave her skin the bliss of his mouth, making her ache— actually *ache*—for more contact.

'My ears…' he said, as he licked one of hers. It made her feel so faint that she spun around just to seek his mouth.

He didn't give it to her, though.

Instead, he went over to her little kitchen window and closed the blind, and then to the living area, and she heard the blinds being closed in there. Finally, he returned to the kitchen.

'We don't want to offend the neighbours,' Alistair said, with a look in his eye that made her blood start to sing.

'No…'

It would not be accidental sex, Libby knew.

Nor would it be just a kiss that went too far, or touches that got out of hand.

It was going to be absolutely, thoroughly, deliciously premeditated—on both sides.

In response, she slipped off her robe as easily as if she were alone and about to step into the shower.

Just slipped it off. Because it hindered what was to come.

Alistair took out a packet of condoms from his pocket and placed them on the bench, his dark eyes so intense in their hold on hers that she felt as if they had already had sex, or were having sex, or had known each other intimately before…many, many times.

'Come here,' he said, even though she was barely a step away.

She went gladly, wrapping her arms around his neck, and drank him in—actually *inhaled* his scent as she slid her hands inside his jumper in order to feel his skin.

And then she pulled the fine fabric of his jumper up, and he continued the motion to strip it off. Libby caught sight of a fan of black hair, and never had she been so bold or so desperate for a man.

She stood on tiptoes to revel in the sensation of his chest against hers, his warm skin on her naked breasts. His kiss was rough, and so thorough, so direct. And the turn-on was so instant that it felt as if they were resuming where they had left things the other night.

Only this time Libby was naked. And from the hips up so was he.

He reached down to unzip himself and she felt dizzy with lust as she held him, impatient to feel him, to have him inside her, in a way she had never anticipated such pleasure before. *Ever.*

'Alistair...'

She was urgent, almost climbing up him in her desperation to coil herself around him, but thank goodness for his Mr Sensible side, because he was taking out a condom from the packet.

Libby watched as he slid it on and found herself panting a little, reaching to touch him.

'You *really* have no patience,' Alistair said, brushing her hand away, making her wait.

She sobbed in relief when he lifted her—but not onto the bench. He carried her over to the fridge that had somehow introduced them.

Certainly it was introducing her to a whole new world—because she was *not* a sex in the kitchen kind of girl.

Nor had she known herself to plead before, but the cold metal on her back as he took her, and the warmth of him against her skin, and the urgency of them together, was a cocktail of sensations that stripped bare all her inhibitions.

'Oh, God...' she said as he ground into her, taking her fast. So fast that it was breathtaking.

And then there were no more words. And there was not a thing she had to do but hold on.

'I'm going to come,' Alistair warned.

'Me...' she said, unable to precede it with *and*.

But he knew what she meant anyway, because he could feel how taut she was in his arms, how close to the edge she was.

'And then I'm going to take you again, so slow...'

Alistair held her so firmly that there was no thought in her head that she might slip, no discomfort, just sheer luxury. That he could bring her to the edge of orgasm like that...as if he already knew every inch of her skin...

Then he moaned, and she arched as he shot into her. She came at his summons, deep and urgent, and then felt a weak relief as it receded. As if it had been essential...

He was breathing hard, and she was panting and resting her head on his shoulder, and then she gave a soft laugh and so did he—a happy, soft laugh, as if to say, *Thank goodness!*

She was glad they hadn't eaten first, because now they had the prospect of a delicious curry waiting for them.

He lowered her down and kissed her, long and slow.

And Libby felt...right.

So right.

As if the move to London made sense now. Because if she hadn't moved then she would never have known him.

That was how right she felt.

'I'm hungry,' Libby said.

'We won't even need to microwave it,' Alistair replied.

No, because it had been so deliciously fast.

'Go and make up the bed,' he suggested. 'We can eat there.'

How could those words make her so happy when making up the sofa-bed was surely the worst job in the world?

But she couldn't stop smiling while he served up dinner, anticipating the pleasure of him climbing in with her.

Alistair gave the naans a little spin in the microwave, and while he did, brought her through a mug of bubbly wine.

'I do have nice glasses,' she told him as she sipped on it, 'but they're in storage.' And then she couldn't help adding, 'You're so sexy…'

'*We* are,' he said, and headed back into the kitchen, giving her a view of his very nice bum.

Oh, she'd wake up in a moment, Libby thought as she lay there. She'd wake up and be in her dressing gown, lying on the sofa, starving hungry and contemplating whether to head to the shops…

Instead, her sexy paramedic returned with dinner and climbed in beside her.

'What are you doing?' he asked, when she pinched his arm.

'Just making sure.'

'Me too…' Alistair said, and he lightly pinched her back, his warm fingers on her breast.

The curry was spicier than she was used to—so much so that she had to reach for the box of tissues and blow her nose.

'Have you slept all day?' Libby asked as they ate.

'A couple of hours this morning.'

They chatted a bit about work, but eventually brought the conversation naturally around to talking about them.

'Perfect Peter?' Libby said. 'I can see where you got your nickname.'

He gave her a curious look.

'So beautiful…' she sighed, looking at his lovely mouth and tracing his features with her fingers, wanting to imprint the shape of him on her soul.

'Libby,' he said, removing her fingers and holding her hand, 'they're being sarcastic.' He frowned, as if he thought she must surely be joking. 'They call me that because I'm so pedantic.'

'Pedantic?'

'Yes—and I'm big on following protocol. Believe me when I say it's not a term of endearment.'

'Well, I think it is,' Libby said. 'I like my paramedics pedantic.'

She thought back to the way he always made his notes, and how he had told her he liked to study rather than chat during breaks.

'I take it all very seriously—maybe too seriously,' he said. 'But I didn't give up law to make friends.'

'You studied law?'

'More than studied. I worked in contract law.'

'How old are you?' Libby asked.

'Thirty-three. You?'

'I told you—twenty-eight.'

'And a half,' he said. 'That's right, you did.'

'That's quite a career change.'

'Yes.'

She looked over at him, waiting for him to elaborate, but he said no more. There was a slight strain in the silence, which felt unusual after the way they communicated together.

'Was being a paramedic something you always wanted to do, or…?' Her voice faded into another stretch of silence.

'No,' Alistair said finally. 'I'd never considered paramedicine. But someone close to me died and I was there…'

'I'm sorry.'

'Asthma,' he added. 'There was nothing I could do. I didn't know what to do. I've never felt so helpless. In truth, I think I had a bit of a meltdown afterwards. We were…' He stopped.

'Tell me,' Libby said.

But he remained silent.

'You were…?' she persisted. 'Married, or engaged, or…? Honestly,' she said, 'I won't mind.'

'Won't mind what?'

'Well, if she was the love of your life. I mean…'

'*He* was my best friend,' Alistair said.

'Oh! Gosh, I'm sorry. How dreadful.'

'It was. It turned out that he hadn't been using his inhalers and had ignored all the signs. There was a group of us. Middle of nowhere.'

'Alistair!' She felt tears in her eyes at the awful thought of what it must have been like.

'Oh, you don't mind now, do you?' Alistair said, and then he surprised her with a smile. 'You jealous little shrew!'

'I am not,' Libby said as he leaned over her and kissed her jealous lips.

But she was one big burning blush, because she had been caught out—one bonk in—for liking him so much. For liking him so, so much…

'Yes.' He took her wrists and held them up, and she squirmed under his scrutiny even as they both smiled. 'Why did you assume it was a woman who had died? The love of my life?'

'I just wanted to know what I was up against,' she admitted. 'Any big relationships before?'

'No,' Alistair said, 'not really. I'm not romantic enough, apparently. I just want sex, sex and more sex…'

'Poor thing,' Libby said, smiling as he kissed her breast.

'How about you?' he asked.

'No big ones either. Well, maybe one…'

She took a breath. She didn't know how to start talking about the details of her recent break-up. And it was surely too soon to be discussing her malfunctioning ovaries! But her troubles had certainly shown Vince in his true colours, so Libby attempted to explain sans details.

'I tend to go for bastards—well, present company excepted, of course…'

'Thank you very much.'

She didn't really know how to describe her ex, because even the longest, most serious relationship of her life had never felt as vital as what she was feeling now for Alistair.

But in the end she didn't have to say anything. His lips were too busy for her own to form words, and his mouth was trailing down her torso and kissing her stomach, first with tenderness, and then with such passion that she whimpered for him to move lower.

Libby and Alistair fell ridiculously fast.

Yet it felt necessarily so.

They didn't leave her sofa-bed for four days.

Only to collect the food they ordered to be delivered.

When she quickly dressed one day, and video called her mother, he stayed well away in the kitchen.

They chatted for a while, mainly about her mother's upcoming birthday, and Alistair could tell they were close. In fact, hearing Libby talking with her parents made him wistful for his own family, and how good he had once believed his relationship with them had been.

Only, it had turned out that the closeness he'd had with his father had been contingent upon him toeing the family line.

Leaving a successful career in law had cost Alistair a lot—and not just financially. The real hit had been the reaction of his family.

It was lonely at the bottom…

'I have to go, Mum,' Libby was saying. 'Kisses…'

They also left the sofa-bed to shower—unfortunately not together, because the cubicle was so tiny, though they did try. Several times.

On the last night before they returned to work Alistair unashamedly watched as Libby showered and told him about the acting lessons she wanted to take.

'Don't laugh.'

'I'm not laughing.' He smiled as, head down, she started to shave her legs. 'I want a front row seat when you perform, though…'

He saw the razor in her hand pause mid-stroke, above her calf, as he referenced the future, but then she sighed and made light of the situation.

'I might never get a part.'

Oh she'd be leading lady, Alistair thought, lost in visions of himself sitting through some dreadful amateur production… And yet, bizarrely, he couldn't pretend he wasn't looking forward to doing just that.

Then it was his turn to shower, and when he came out she told him he looked incredible— even with her lemon-coloured daisy-embroidered towel wrapped around his hips.

* * *

The towel that covered her entire torso was like a hand towel on him, thought Libby, and she didn't want this magical time to be ending.

She'd wanted to look up when he'd spoken about front row seats—to say that she'd make sure he got them and she wanted flowers in her dressing room too...

Was she being ridiculous and reading too much into his words?

Or was Alistair feeling the same?

'I don't want to go to work tomorrow,' Libby admitted.

She was kneeling behind him, drying his shoulders, but she stopped what she was doing and proceeded to wet them again with her mouth.

'We're going,' he said, and turned his head to meet her lips. Then he turned around more completely and pressed her down, so she lay beneath him.

It would have been far more comfortable for them to have relocated to his home for this four-day period, because he had a bigger bed—and a bigger shower, for that matter—but as he stared down at Libby, Alistair knew why they hadn't.

His practical mind was bewildered, because

he had the feeling that if he ever took her back to his—well, they would return to Libby's flat for the sole purpose of collecting her things.

It terrified him that moving her into his place actually felt as if it might be the sensible thing to do.

He was usually so closed to others. He thought things through...

But, looking down at her now, Alistair felt as if he had Libby's dizzy, impulsive head on his shoulders—and he wanted nothing more than to take her back to his home and keep her there.

To be swept up in such a tide both unnerved and thrilled him. The feelings she provoked in him were so new, so unfamiliar, that he felt it would be necessary to examine them in more detail when he was alone.

And yet at the same time he did not want to come up for air.

Did not want to leave, nor for normal services to resume.

He liked this new normal.

No—he *loved* this new normal.

Libby felt the burn of his stare and saw something she had never seen in a lover's eyes before—something so deep that it felt almost like the L word.

She was not going to ruin things by blurting

that out, so she just put her hand to his head and pulled his face down to hers.

He kissed her deeply, and she squirmed beneath him, because he was rough and unshaven after four days away from his razor.

One more kiss, she thought. Just one more...

But it was already one kiss too many, because they were in over their heads. Neither wanted their four-day sex-fest to end—and it was temptation at its purest to try to extend their time away from reality, to pretend that outside pressures didn't exist, that nothing bad could ever happen as long as they were together...

Alistair was reaching for the box of condoms.

'Last one,' he told her.

'Poor you,' Libby said.

'Why?' he asked as she slid it on.

'You'll have to go to the petrol station on such a cold night...'

They really were in trouble, she thought. They were both so close to tearing up the rule book...to saying no more condoms and moving in together...to succumbing to desire and moving from the *crazy about you* phase to the *I love you* one.

Don't spoil it, Libby told herself and closed her eyes.

Then she moaned as he filled her.

'Oh, God,' Alistair said on an exhale.

'There,' Libby said—unnecessarily, because he already knew.

They couldn't even part long enough for him to go to the petrol station when they were ready again, and so, in the absence of supplies, Libby woke him intimately with her mouth.

It was complete and utter bliss…

But of course paradise had to come to an end eventually.

'I don't want to go work,' Libby said again, at six-thirty the next morning.

She had just showered, and had come out of the bathroom to the sight of him sexy and un-shaven and pulling on his clothes.

Extremely reluctantly she dressed too. 'And you're on till when?' she asked, pouting.

'Midnight,' Alistair said. 'Well, depending on what time we get our last job.'

'The off-duty rota hates us.'

'It's been pretty good to us, really,' he said, dunking tea bags into two mugs. 'We haven't left your sofa-bed in four days.'

'Why did I say I'd go home to my parents on my next days off?'

'Because it's your mother's sixtieth!' Alistair smiled.

'Oh, yes…' *And those bloody tests.*

He gave her one last lingering kiss.

'Drop your glove so you have to come back,' she said into his sexy mouth.

'No.'

'Please can we call in sick?'

'No!'

He was by far too responsible, Libby thought, as he peeled her off him and with a smile headed off.

Well, he was by far too responsible *except* for that damn bike, Libby amended when she heard the engine, and no doubt he was annoying all her neighbours with the noise.

It was a ten-minute walk to work—twenty when it was freezing and you stopped for coffee and a doughnut on the way. Actually, a *bag* of doughnuts, because May had sulked last time when Libby had mentioned she'd had one and not got some for everyone.

'Good morning, Libby.' May smiled. 'Is it snowing outside?'

'No…' Libby frowned, but when she got to the changing room she laughed as she understood May's little joke. Taking off her coat, she saw that it was covered in icing sugar and, when she looked in the mirror, so was her face. She rinsed herself off and changed into scrubs. She was all floaty, floaty, happy, happy…

'Filthy morning out there. We're going to be

snowed under.' May rolled her eyes and pulled her cardigan around her. 'Did you see the icing sugar?'

'I did!' Libby laughed. 'Don't worry, I bought a whole bag of doughnuts to share.'

'Good lass! You're learning.'

'Yes—either hide the evidence or buy plenty for all...'

'You're very chipper this morning,' May said as they waited for handover.

'Chipper?'

'Cheery,' May translated.

Indeed Libby was.

At least until the Bat Phone interrupted handover.

'Car versus motorbike...'

It was the cyclist they were being alerted about, and the mobile intensive care unit was attending.

'No ETA yet,' said May, summoning the trauma team, and Libby found herself in Resus, trying to tame her irrational mind.

Because Alistair had left her place ages ago.

She looked at the time and worked out that it must have been thirty or forty minutes ago.

Oh, God, it actually could be him.

It really could be Alistair involved in the accident.

Libby felt sick to her stomach as she set up for their incoming guest.

The trauma team came in, asking for more information, and May told them the little she knew as Libby ran through an IV, her heart hammering in her chest.

It remained hammering when the phone buzzed again.

'Okay,' May said. 'Thank you for letting us know.' She replaced the receiver and turned to the awaiting team. 'We've been stood down,' she told them. 'Declared dead on scene.'

It was horrible. Watching the trauma team disperse…looking down at all the equipment that had been set up and now would not be used because the patient hadn't made it in.

Libby's heart was still hammering.

She'd always hated motorbikes—well, since the start of her nursing days—but never more so than now.

'How old was the patient?' Libby asked.

'They didn't say.'

She felt sick.

Truly.

She kept wanting to text Alistair, to ask if he was okay, but she thought of her mother, who always did just that, and how much it annoyed her.

She refused to be like that, even though her heart felt as if it were in her throat.

It wasn't long before the driver of the car was brought in, and the poor lady was beside herself. 'I didn't see him,' she sobbed over and over. 'I didn't see him…'

'Vera,' Libby said, 'let us take care of you.'

She was trying to calm the patient, and at the same time attempting to undress her and complete a set of observations on the shocked lady.

She held her arm as they got IV access. 'Try and stay still. Your husband's on his way.'

'I'm not even hurt.'

'You *are* hurt,' Libby said.

Though her injuries were relatively minor, Vera herself was broken inside. She lay on her back with a hard collar around her neck, choking on tears of shock and regret. Libby wiped the lady's tears away and did her best to be there with her patient's emotions. Vera's world had changed for ever.

May put her head in and nudged Libby to come out. 'The police are here. And Huba's going to assess her. I need you over in Resus.'

May was correct with her prediction—it did turn out to be a very busy morning. When May suggested she go for coffee, Libby glanced at the time, surprised to see that it was almost eleven.

'Are you okay, Libby?' May checked.

'Of course.'

'Only, you look like a little ghost.'

She felt like one.

She had a horrible, haunted feeling that she couldn't shake.

The coffee didn't help, and nor did a slice of dark chocolate cake.

Part of her knew that it hadn't been him.

Surely word would have come from one of the other paramedics by now.

Of course it would have.

The morning had given her such a fright—and not just because of the motorcycle accident. It was more that her sense of panic had been so intense.

She had never fallen this hard for anyone.

Not even close.

It was scary, actually.

She honestly hadn't come up for air since they'd met. One minute she'd been crying over her ovaries, and then…

He'd revved into her life.

Claimed her with a kiss.

When she'd left work the other day she had known she fancied him, wanted him, and that much she'd thought she could handle. But now she had returned to work with her feelings in a completely new order.

Alistair Lloyd had shot straight to the top.

Libby felt as if a thief had been in and taken her heart, stamped *Alistair* upon it and then put it back in her chest.

He'd be perfect if it weren't for that bike.

Seriously perfect.

So perfect that it troubled her.

Don't fall too hard, she warned herself as she headed back to the department.

But it felt like closing the stable door four days after the horse had bolted—actually, six days, given how incredible their first kiss had been the night of the fridge-moving.

It had been a long day, and Libby felt exhausted, but suddenly there Alistair was, making up the stretcher as Brendan handed their patient over to May. Libby did an abrupt about-turn—and not just to get the wine Alistair had so thoughtfully bought for her to give back to him.

She needed to calm herself.

She'd felt such a flood of relief to see for herself that he was okay, and an even bigger flood of relief that she hadn't texted him with her fears.

Get a grip, she told herself, before heading back out there with the wine.

'Alistair!' she called, and made her way over. 'This is for you,' she said, handing it over. She hoped she sounded casual enough. 'Thank you so much for your help with the fridge.'

'You didn't have to do that,' Alistair said. 'That's very considerate of you.'

'What's going on?' Brendan was all cheery as he walked over with a blanket. 'Oh, you got your wine.'

'Yes,' Alistair said.

'Have you invited Libby to your leaving drinks?'

'I'm not having any leaving drinks,' Alistair said, rolling his eyes as he took the blanket and Brendan headed down to Reception to register the patient. 'He's trying to give me a helping hand.'

'How so?' Libby frowned, a little confused.

'Brendan's got it into his head that I like you, and because I don't tell him all the details of my private life he's trying to matchmake.'

'Oh!'

'He thinks I'm shy.'

'Boy, have I got news for Brendan!' Libby chuckled. 'So, what's this about a leaving do?'

'I got a call just a moment ago. I've been accepted into HART.'

'Is that…?' She swallowed. 'Is that the hazardous incident response thing?'

Brendan returned and happily answered her

question. 'He's aiming to get into tactical response.'

'Eventually,' Alistair amended.

'Terrorism, guns...'

Brendan was like a kid, making a gun with two fingers and pretending to shoot like a cowboy. Usually Libby would have laughed. Not today.

'Alistair will be right in the thick of it, lucky bugger.'

'Seriously?' Libby tried to hide the look of horror that she knew must have swept over her features, but Alistair was still making up the stretcher so he didn't notice. 'How's that lucky?

'I'd do it if I could—not that I'd pass the physical,' Brendan sighed. 'But if I were ten years younger...'

'When do you start?' Libby asked Alistair.

'Soon. They've got me on the next intake. Six weeks residential.'

'Oh.'

Libby just stood there and tried to push out an appropriate or normal-sounding response.

'Congratulations,' she managed.

She tried to remember that she wasn't supposed to know him well—at least in front of Brendan and other colleagues—because it was all just too new to share.

'Thanks,' Alistair said neutrally, as if she were just another co-worker.

Brendan, though, was persistent with his matchmaking. 'So, if I can persuade him to have leaving drinks, can we count you in?'

'Sure,' Libby said, even while thinking, *Not a chance in hell.*

No way would she celebrate this!

'Come on, Brendan. Time to go.' Alistair rolled his eyes at his matchmaker. 'Thanks for the wine, Libby.'

No, no, no, no, no...

It was like being in a nightmare. And it would be even more of a nightmare if she got involved with him.

She was already involved—she couldn't deny that. But if she became seriously involved it would actually be her worst nightmare to have the man she loved working in such a dangerous profession.

She'd be like her mother...constantly glued to the news.

This morning his motorbike had been her only problem, Libby thought as she took the Tube home and then forced herself to go to the shop.

After all the unhealthy food they'd eaten, she'd buy a salad for her supper. And some chicken parmigiana, because it came in a pack of two—but would that be enough for Alistair?

She stared at the chicken parmigiana for two and it scared her how easily she had factored him in...how her head, mind and body all wanted and craved his company tonight.

Usually, with other men, she'd be wondering whether he'd call when his shift ended, but instead she had assumed—or rather *knew*—that he would. She was confident that Alistair considered what they had found together as wonderful as she did.

But for sanity's sake she must end things with Alistair right now. Mustn't she? Wasn't that the best course of action?

Yet she bought dinner for two, while telling herself she would eat the spare chicken tomorrow night.

Then she bought soap.

And then she looked at the condoms and didn't know whether to throw a pack in.

And then she looked at the tampons—but she had plenty at home because it had been ages since her last period...

Oh, yes. That whole thing.

Libby took out her phone and looked at the GP app and then the texts asking her to confirm her tests. They felt frighteningly close.

Alistair had asked why she and Vince had

broken up and she hadn't known what to say...
knowing it was too soon to get into talking
about her ovaries.

She had wanted to confide in him but had
held back.

Libby wasn't sure she wanted such a conversation.

It all felt too much.

She felt too much.

She wanted to call him and beg him not to
take the job with HART, beg him to get rid
of the bike, and confide in him that she was
scared about going home for these tests.

She was feeling things she had never experienced before.

The edge of love?

If that was the case...well, you don't try to
change the person you love.

That much, Libby knew.

*Please be my usual type of bastard and don't
call*, Libby thought as she trudged home. *Or,
if you do call, please give me the sense to end
things.*

When she arrived home her flat was in
chaos. It had made her smile that morning, but
now it made her heart ache as she tidied all evidence of *them* away, and then spent an hour researching the line of work he wished to pursue.

It made her feel rather ill.

Libby heated the chicken parmigiana, but couldn't even finish her single one, so it went into the fridge next to his. Then she pulled her sofa-bed out and made it.

The worst job in the world?

Not any more.

Alistair's new job was, for Libby, the worst job in the world.

For her.

She would be saved from making a decision tonight, Libby thought as time passed, midnight came and went, and she didn't hear from him.

She thought about his professional, neutral approach to her at work today. Perhaps he wasn't feeling it quite as much as she, after all?

Then, just before one a.m., her phone bleeped a message. She didn't open it, but it flashed up on her watch so it was impossible to ignore.

Are you up?

Of course she was up!

Furthermore, if she continued seeing Alistair then she'd be perpetually up...worrying.

She was her mother's daughter after all.

And that was why she couldn't get further involved.

She didn't answer his text.

She mustn't.

Instead, she lay in the dark and thought of another old saying, one she wished she'd heeded: *Look before you leap...*

Foolishly, she hadn't.

It was odd to break up with someone because you liked them too much—or so much that the knot in your chest was pulled tight at the thought of them on a bike or working at a dangerous job. So much, that you might have to tell them you were having fertility investigations, because the outcome might actually matter to them.

Thursday dawned, and as Libby made a chicken parmigiana sandwich to take for supper on her late shift, it was her mother, rather than Alistair, that called—all worried about something she'd seen on the news.

'I'm fine,' Libby told her. 'What are you talking about?' She held in a sigh as her mother told her about a missing person she'd heard about on the news. 'Mum, that's not even close to where I live. London's a pretty big place, you know...' She took a breath. 'Of course you had to be sure that I was fine...'

Libby, while weary of her mother's constant anxiety, perhaps better understood now. After all, she'd immediately panicked that Alistair might be the motorcyclist who had died…

At least her mother had a reason to live on her nerves. She had lost a child before Libby had been born and a catastrophising nature had ensued.

And Libby would do everything in her power not to live like that…

Just as she'd finished packing up her sandwiches Alistair called.

As she had known he would.

'Alistair…' she took a breath '…my phone's playing up. I just saw your text…' She was too good a liar.

'I'm at work, so I can't talk,' Alistair told her. 'But I should be finished by seven, if you want to come over to mine after work?'

'Alistair.' Libby halted him quickly, otherwise she knew that she would give in to temptation. Especially as he was inviting her to his home…pulling her closer when she was trying to break away before things got too intertwined. 'I can't tonight…' She took a breath. 'I'm wiped.'

She loathed confrontation of any sort—just avoided it at all costs—but, more importantly, she didn't want to do this. She *couldn't* do this right now.

'Is everything okay?' Alistair checked, perhaps hearing the strain in her voice.

'I guess, but… Look, you're going away soon, and…' She swallowed. 'I just don't think…' She didn't know what to say. 'I'm dreadful at long-distance relationships…'

That made her sound flaky, and incapable of effort—as if all she wanted was a good time. But it was better that he think that than know the real reason why she had to end things before they became any more serious.

Libby persisted with that line. 'I don't see the point when it's all just going to fizzle out.'

'I'm only going away for six weeks.'

'I know, but—'

'It's fine,' he clipped. 'You don't have to explain.' He was being supremely polite, but then suddenly he seemed confused, or perhaps cross. 'Are you *serious*, Libby?'

'Yes.' Libby said it with more conviction than she felt, and then, possibly already realising the utter error of her ways, she wanted to soften it…retract it, perhaps…

But the line had already gone dead.

He had ended the call.

She stared at his name on her phone for a very long time, fighting the urge to call him back, but then she took a breath and hit *Delete* on his name and number.

And then, because she knew she was weak, especially where Alistair was concerned, she emptied the deleted items too.

It felt wrong.

So wrong that she was filled with a sudden vision of herself at the phone shop, pleading with them to work some magic to retrieve his number.

But it was already done.

And what was worse…

She regretted it already.

CHAPTER THREE

IT WAS AWFUL.

Far, far worse than any break-up she had known before.

Usually Libby phoned a friend, went out and had a glass of wine and bemoaned her situation, then came home and watched her favourite film in the world while working her way through a bar of chocolate.

Sometimes she had to use the friend, chocolate and film technique for several nights, but it didn't help here.

There was nothing to bemoan about Alistair, and she didn't feel as if her friends back in Norfolk would understand.

Still Libby tried. She was desperate for insight, and so confused by her feelings and her handling of things, that she called Olivia.

'How's London?' Olivia asked.

'Great,' Libby said. 'Well, actually…' She

hesitated. 'I met someone and we've just broken up...'

'You've only just got there! It can't have been that serious...'

Libby heard Little Timothy, crying to be fed, and could almost feel Olivia's distraction.

'I really liked him,' she said.

'So what happened?'

'It's complicated,' Libby said, but then heard Timothy's screams quadruple. 'I've caught you at a bad time.'

'Hey, you're home in a few days...we can catch up then. Well, if I can get a babysitter...'

'Sure.'

'Or you could come over.'

A night with Olivia and her husband and new baby really wouldn't be the balm for a broken heart that she was after. Especially after she'd had a barrage of fertility tests...

She tried to read *Wuthering Heights*, because that always pulled her in, but, no, it wasn't working.

So she tried watching her favourite film version of it, but even that didn't spirit her away tonight; it just made her cry.

She also had a dreadful sick feeling, and she couldn't even make a cup of tea without thinking of him, because when she went to get milk from the fridge she felt as if she could see their reflection in the stainless steel.

Even her daisy-covered towel made her weep.

Work was…

Difficult.

Everything still felt incredibly new, with all the different consultants and registrars, and today, just when she felt she'd got a handle on who the junior doctors were, their rotation changed and a new intake started.

More new faces.

Then Brendan brought in a patient, but the leap of her heart was halted when she saw he was working with a woman.

Another new face.

'Lina!' May said to Brendan's partner, 'You're back!'

'Thank goodness,' Brendan said. 'Can you imagine a whole set of shifts with Perfect Peter endlessly quoting policy?'

'God love him,' May laughed. 'He *is* very thorough.'

Libby would have liked to shout at them, but of course she didn't. Not only because she and Alistair had remained a secret, but more because she loathed any sort of confrontation.

For herself, she loved how much care he took

to do things right when it came to safe working procedures.

Worse than not seeing him, though, was the moment when she did.

He'd had his hair cut, and was so clean-shaven she wanted to put up her hand and feel his jaw.

Not here.

Maybe tonight?

But no, of course she couldn't. Because she had ended things.

If she hadn't messed up, she might even have felt it this morning.

Oh, what had she done?

Not that it seemed to have affected him in the least. Alistair was treating her exactly as he always had at work, and exactly as he treated everyone else.

No more, no less.

'Morning, Libby,' he greeted her. 'This is...'

And he introduced his patient and gave her a diligent handover, treating her exactly as he might have May or Dianne...

It was Libby who was one big burning blush and a stumbling mess.

'Alistair.' She caught him as he was heading out. 'Could I borrow you for a moment?' She smiled to the paramedic he was working with today—an apologetic smile that asked for a private word.

'What's this about?' Alistair asked.

'A patient you brought in last week…'

He frowned, but nodded to his colleague, who left them to it.

'What patient?' he asked.

'It's not about a patient,' she admitted.

'In that case…' Alistair shook his head. 'I'm at work, Libby,' he said. 'I don't bring my private life here.'

And he walked off. Just like that.

Libby had to fight not to run after him, to call him back, to plead with him to bring his private life to work so that she could admit she had made the most dreadful mistake.

Instead she just stood there and watched him leave.

There was no relief during her visit back home to her parents in Norfolk.

In the familiar streets she felt like a different person from the one who had left. The woman who had lived here hadn't known Alistair, or the bliss that had awaited her.

But she had to be happy and 'up, up, up' for her mother's sixtieth celebrations. It was quite a party, and Libby laughed and danced the night away.

On Sunday she went out with friends from her theatre group...yet she already felt out of the loop because, although it was great to see them, they mainly spoke about their new production.

Every day she felt worse about her decision to end things with Alistair rather than better.

Even so, there were confirmations that perhaps she had made the right choice, because on the Monday she had her detailed ultrasound and loads of blood tests.

Even though she was an emergency nurse, Libby couldn't stand the sight of blood when it was her own. She felt a bit faint, afterwards, and sat down outside and had a drink of water, deciding some chocolate might be required to replace all the iron. She was feeling so light-headed that she came the closest yet to caving and calling the station Alistair was based at and asking him to contact her.

To say she was so sorry and had made a ridiculous mistake.

And please, don't take that job...

Oh, and can you get rid of your bike please?

And, in the interests of full disclosure, before you change your life because I ask you to, you should know I'm going to be a mess any day soon if I find out I can't get pregnant...

Her feelings couldn't survive the real word,

Libby decided. And when she got home from the shopping trip she'd pretended to be on she found her mother was pacing because her father hadn't called her back.

Oh, heavens!

That would have been Libby's future if she had stayed with Alistair. She had already been like her that morning, when the motorcyclist had died before reaching A&E, and that had been enough of a glimpse into her possible future...

And Olivia was no help when they finally caught up—at her home, because she hadn't been able to get a babysitter.

'How long were you seeing him exactly?' she asked.

'Six days. Six perfect days.'

'So perfect that you ended it?' she said, sounding perplexed.

'I panicked,' Libby admitted. 'What with his new job and the motorbike and...' She paused. 'And I didn't know how to tell him about all these tests I'm having.'

'Isn't it a bit early for all that?' Olivia gently suggested. 'Look, I know that Vince was awful about it, but you haven't even seen the gynaecologist yet. There might not even be a problem.'

Said she, a woman who was holding her new baby in her arms…

It had been horrible, going through all those tests alone—as if her potential problem didn't count quite as much because she didn't have a partner in tow.

As if, because she wasn't actively trying to get pregnant, it was a problem for later and didn't matter much.

Yet to Libby it did.

And she couldn't talk to her mother about it, because she couldn't talk to her mother about anything problematic lest it upset her.

Then there came a different sort of lonely when, late the next afternoon, she stepped off the train in London and took the Tube, then walked down the high street, wondering if every passing ambulance might be him.

Instead of heading straight to her little flat, which just reminded her of Alistair, she stopped to get coffee and some doughnuts.

'There you go, Libby,' the barista said as he handed over her coffee.

'Oh, thank you.' She blinked in confusion because she'd been daydreaming.

'Two doughnuts today?' he checked.

'I'm starving!'

One now and one later.

Or one now and one straight after.

But then she realised why he was delaying her order.

'Do you want to go for a drink some time?' he asked.

No, she didn't. She wanted coffee and doughnuts and to cry all over again. But maybe she *should* go. Maybe a drink and a night out with…

Liam. That was his name. Or was it Leo?

'Sounds great,' she said.

He told her about a pub where the music was good—hopefully loud enough that he wouldn't notice if she got his name wrong, she thought.

It was just a drink.

A drink with someone who had a nice safe job.

Someone wouldn't leave her heart in knots and a crazed feeling in her brain.

So instead of spending the evening home alone, she pulled on a cheerful wraparound dress, strappy sandals with high heels and then, because that was a rather summery ensemble for February, added a coat.

It's just a drink, Libby told herself again as she sat on the Tube.

But not with Alistair.

She stepped off the Tube onto an unfamiliar platform and clipped her way along in her heels, all the time knowing it wasn't where she wanted to be…

She thought of their lovely, single date—the one time she had gone out with Alistair. Of how they'd had pepper steak and wedges, and he'd bought her a chocolate egg while she got bread and milk…and how utterly perfect he had been.

She got on the escalator to go up to the surface. It was steep, one of the old wooden ones, and for some reason that caused her eyes to fill with tears and she was momentarily blinded.

He'd probably left for his new job already— or he would be going next week.

Would Brendan and Lina even know where he was? And if she asked would they give her his number?

What the hell was she doing, going out with someone else when she was crying on an escalator over the most stupid mistake of her life?

She didn't for a second want things to be over with Alistair.

And she would tell him so. Yes, she would. Right now.

Libby turned to go back down the stairs— though of course she wasn't on stairs.

She was standing halfway up a very steep escalator…

It was odd to know no more than that.

CHAPTER FOUR

EVERYTHING REALLY WAS most odd, Libby thought.

'Alistair?'

He was here?

And in uniform?

Those chocolaty velvety eyes were staring down at her and she knew it was the only place she wanted to be—back in the path of his gaze.

Only she didn't know why she was…

'Alistair?'

She was starting to panic as it dawned on her that she was at work…but lying down. Actually, she was in Resus—and furthermore May was taking her blood pressure. And, just to confuse things even more, Alistair really was here.

It didn't make sense.

Nothing made sense.

'Hey,' he said. 'You're okay.'

'Why am I here?' She watched as he glanced

over to May, who stood on the opposite side of her. 'Alistair, how come *you're* here?'

'Because I was bringing a patient in when you arrived,' he said patiently. 'Libby, do you know where you are?'

She looked at the white ceiling and the bright lights and heard all the monitors bleeping away. It really wasn't hard to guess. 'Work.'

'Do you remember what happened?'

Not really...

Yet as she lay there Libby found herself chasing wisps of a conversation she'd had with May—one during which she'd been trying to sit up and go home and May had been insisting that now wasn't the time.

'I fell?' Libby said hesitantly, unsure if the conversation with May had even taken place.

'Yes.'

'Are you the paramedic who brought me in?' Libby asked, and saw that he'd closed his eyes for a second, as if he was slightly frustrated by her question, even though she thought it was an obvious one.

She had no clue that she'd asked it many times before...

'No,' Alistair said. 'It wasn't me. I was here with a patient when they brought you in, and I came over to see if you were okay.'

'I'm fine,' Libby bristled, embarrassed and

unsure as she looked up at May. 'I'd like to go home.'

'Not yet, Libby. Your parents are on their way.'

'My parents?' *Oh, for God's sake!* 'Why on earth have they been called? My mother will be beside herself...' She tried to sit up, but Alistair held her shoulder. 'Get off me!' she shouted uncharacteristically—not just to Alistair, but also to May, who was trying to get her to lie down as well. 'I want to go home.'

'Libby,' May said, 'you've had quite a fall. You're a bit confused...'

No. I'm not confused, Libby thought.

She was cross. Because someone had called her parents and her mother was going to freak.

'Why did you have to call them?' she demanded of May, and then she glared at Alistair. 'Why are you even here? I'm not your patient...' She knew she was being mean, and she wasn't a mean person. She was also being spiteful and that wasn't her. 'Perfect Peter?' she sneered. 'Not!'

'I'll leave,' Alistair said. 'I'm obviously upsetting her.'

'No, stay!' Libby was suddenly frantic, because it wasn't Alistair who was upsetting her, or May, but everything else—her confusion, her parents' imminent arrival, the fact that she was in Resus, with a huge collar around her neck, and absolutely no idea how she'd ended up here.

Or why.

Neither did she know why she was being horrible to Alistair when she wanted him to stay more than anything else.

The only certainty she knew was that she and Alistair had broken up and she did not deserve his concern—and yet it would seem that she had it anyway.

He was holding her hand gently, but she was gripping his, clinging on to it for dear life. '*Am* I confused?' she asked him. Because she trusted him. He was pedantic, and she knew he would tell her the truth.

'Yes,' he said. 'You are.'

'How do you know that?'

'Because you keep asking me the same questions and you've been quite combative...'

'Me?'

'Yes.' He offered her a kind smile. 'You're getting better though. You're more coherent now.'

'You should go back to your partner then,' Libby said, assuming that whoever he was working with this evening must be outside, waiting.

'It's fine. I've already signed off.'

'Why?'

'Because…' He closed his eyes and seemed to be battling to find a suitable response. He seemed upset.

'Why have you signed off?'

'I didn't want you to be on your own. I wanted to stay at least till your parents get here. I was worried about you…'

May cut in then. 'Libby, you were very distressed when you first came in to Resus.'

'How long have I been here?'

'An hour.'

'A whole *hour*?' She frowned.

Although now that she thought about it, it felt like a whole lot more than an hour was unaccounted for. She hadn't just lost her time in the department, but getting here, and the reason why she was here.

'What happened?'

He pressed his lips together and she realised that he *had* been frustrated by her question before.

'Have I already asked that?'

'It's fine.' He gave her hand a little squeeze and she squeezed his back. 'You had a fall on an escalator on the underground.'

That's right, she thought, slowly piecing things together. She'd been on one of the steep wooden ones.

'I was going on a date,' Libby told him. 'With someone who doesn't try to get themselves killed for a living.'

Had she really just said that out loud?

'Good for you,' Alistair said, as if the news wasn't a surprise.

Had he heard her say that before too?

'A date with someone who doesn't ride a motorbike,' she snapped.

'Well, it would seem one of those ridiculous heels you were wearing to impress your date might have got stuck in the escalator, or...'

'No,' she said.

Because that wasn't right. She knew she hadn't got her heel stuck, but she couldn't quite remember what *had* occurred—or rather, she was only remembering parts of it. She remembered lying on the escalator and wondering why it wasn't moving.

'They stopped the escalator...'

'They did.' May smiled and smoothed back her hair. 'You're starting to remember.'

'May?' She looked at her boss, and with little flashes of recall starting to ping in her mind she remembered fighting her off when she'd first arrived in the department. 'I'm sorry...'

'You've nothing to be sorry about,' May said. 'You're going to be fine. Garth wants you to have a head CT and...' She turned to Alistair. 'Could you excuse us a moment?'

Libby felt him let go of her hand. She was embarrassed to be seen like this, but at the same time so glad he was here in this swirly confusing world.

'Do you know the date of your LMP?' asked May, when he'd gone.

'No.' She shook her head. 'But I never do. I'm having some investigations...'

'It's okay,' May said. 'But is there any chance you could be pregnant?'

'I might not ever be,' she said, starting to cry. 'That's why I'm having the investigations.'

'Let's get a urine specimen...just to be sure. I've got a bedpan...'

'God, no.'

'Yes,' May said. 'This is no time to be shy.'

There really wasn't any opportunity to be shy.

Before Libby could insist that she was well enough to walk, a wave of nausea hit her. She tried to sit up and reach for the kidney dish, only the movement felt too violent, and the bay in Resus was so warm, and yet her skin seemed to have turned to ice.

'May...' She started retching and then her vision seemed to split, for there were two versions of everything—even when she closed her eyes.

She was both vomiting and half fainting, and she could feel the push of May's hands again—not just lying her down, but turning her onto her side.

Neither was there time to be embarrassed. Libby was numbly aware that May was pressing the buzzer and summoning help.

'You're okay, Libby,' May told her. 'You just sat up too fast. Here's Garth now…'

Garth was the consultant on duty, and Libby lay, eyes closed, and heard herself being discussed as he peeled open each eye in turn and shone a torch in.

'Libby,' he said, 'do you know where you are?'

'The Primary.'

'And do you know what happened to you?'

'I fell.' She could remember that now.

'You certainly did,' Garth said, and then he asked her to push him away, and then to lift her legs. 'Is CT clear yet?' he asked May.

'Not yet,' she answered.

'Let's give her eight milligrams of Ondansetron…'

He also asked if she knew when her last period had been, or if there was any chance of pregnancy.

'No,' May answered for her. 'I was just about to get a urine sample…'

Libby could hear them talking over her, and about her, but she didn't have the energy to cut in—to explain that she and Alistair had been very careful. It was none of their damned business, her fuzzy mind wanted to shout. But instead she just listened as Garth changed his orders.

'Okay let's give metoclopramide…'

She heard Dianne's voice. 'Her mother's on the phone again.'

'No!' Libby knew she sounded like a drunken sailor. 'She gets so upset…' she tried to explain. 'Dramatic.'

'It's okay, Libby, I'll talk to her,' Garth said. 'May, call CT and see how long they'll be. We'll need to sedate her for the procedure.'

They didn't need to sedate her, Libby was sure, but she shakily signed the consent form. She no longer felt sick, but certainly she didn't want to move even an inch, so she lay there quietly, feeling the nausea receding. She was grateful when May and Dianne changed the bedding and her gown, and for the coolness of a wet cloth on her face.

'They're ready for her now,' Dianne said.

'Let's get her round.'

* * *

Alistair had seen the light flash over Resus, and heard the buzzer summoning staff, so he knew that something must be happening—he just hadn't known what or to whom. But then he had heard 'head injury', and Garth asking May to hurry along CT.

That was when he had felt the grip of panic that had hit him when Libby had first arrived tighten like a vice.

He'd just been finishing his notes on a patient when she'd arrived. Ironically, it was the patient who was holding up CT now, because he had been taken straight there.

Libby had been shouting, crying, terrified and confused when she'd arrived. He'd never heard her shout, and yet he had recognised her cries instantly and looked up.

She hadn't recognised him.

Or May, whom he'd assisted in holding Libby down as she'd attempted to flee.

She'd been in an alternative world when she'd arrived. One where pelicans—which apparently she was terrified of—roamed the moors. And where her name was Cathy and she wanted to say things differently.

Slowly, over an hour, she'd started to return—but now, just when things had been looking better, those lights had flashed.

May came out. 'We're taking her round to CT…'

'Is she okay?'

'Alistair…' May hesitated.

He knew that there was little she could tell him, since he was not family and they were not a couple.

'We'll know more soon.' She paused mid-stride. 'Why don't you go and wait in the staff-room?'

He shook his head. He could not face the chatter in there. 'I'll just wait here, if that's okay.' But he knew that was impractical…him standing in the busy corridor. 'Or I can go and wait outside.'

'Tell you what—why don't you take a seat in Interview Room Three?' May suggested, but then she had no choice but to dash off to take Libby to CT.

It would be an awful wait, and since he wasn't next of kin or anything, he knew no one would be rushing to inform him of any updates to her condition.

They weren't even together any more, he reminded himself. He had no right to know. And yet he felt as if he needed to know, and he wished he had a right to know.

He had walked more relatives and friends into Interview Room Three than he could count, and it felt surreal to be heading there himself.

'Peter?' Lina said, walking towards him, smiling as she teased him with the use of his nickname. But then her expression changed when she saw his grim expression. 'What's going on?'

'I'm not sure,' he said, possibly sounding as disconnected as Libby had been for the past hour, because he gave no real explanation as he answered. 'She's just been taken for an urgent CT.'

'Are you okay?'

Alistair knew that Lina was as used as he was to having to work out a story from someone who wasn't able to articulate themselves clearly.

'I've been told to wait in here,' he said.

'Have you told Control?' Lina asked, and opened the door of the small, private waiting room.

'Yes, I was on with Rory—he's going out single.'

He didn't need to add that he was too upset to work. Certainly he hadn't told Libby that when she'd asked what he was doing there. But seeing her being wheeled in, dazed, confused and ranting, and not even knowing who he was, let alone where she was, had been more than distressing. He hadn't let that show to anyone, of course, but he had felt it all the same.

Brendan came over then, and the trio walked into the bland, joyless room. Brendan asked what was happening and Alistair told him his hunch had been right.

'Libby,' he said. 'We were seeing each other.'

'I knew it!' Brendan said, delighted to be proved right. 'So what's happened?'

Alistair told them the little he knew, and was grateful that they were waiting with him.

'We broke up,' he said, and then inexplicably found himself saying, 'I'm not sure why. I thought we were going great and then...'

He felt odd. He never confided in colleagues, or even his friends, really—he just didn't do that type of thing. Yet here he was, doing exactly that.

'She thought you called me Perfect Peter because I was, you know...'

'What?' Brendan asked.

'Good-looking.'

'Well, she *is* getting her head examined,' Brendan said, and somehow this made Alistair smile. Lina even held his hand and he let her.

'She was really confused at first,' he went on. 'But I thought she getting better. She'd been ranting about *Wuthering Heights* and pelicans when she arrived, but she became more lucid. And then something happened. They dashed her off. But I don't if she's had a seizure or blown a pupil...'

'Alistair.' Lina halted him. 'You can't know what's happened, so stop thinking the worst.'

'It's our job to think the worst.'

'The worst' was always amongst the list of possibilities in his head, so that he was prepared for any eventuality. Only this didn't feel like it did when he was at work.

Nothing like this.

It was a lot longer than an hour before May put her head around the door. They were all startled.

'Sorry to give you a fright,' May said, and then asked Brendan and Lina to excuse them for a moment. 'She's okay,' May told him. 'I can't give details, of course, but I can tell you that she's okay. We had to sedate her for the CT, but she's awake now and more lucid. Although she's still quite...' May looked for the right words. 'Out of sorts.'

Her confusion had been fading—he'd seen that for himself—but the frustration and short temper had increased, he was told, though that was common with a recent head injury. He'd seen the panic flare in her eyes as she'd tried to make sense of things, and he'd also seen her effort to remain in control.

'She's been admitted to our obs ward. She might be transferred to Neuro later, but Garth's keeping her here for now.' May looked at him. 'It sounds like you and Libby have quite a lot of unfinished business between you...'

He said nothing.

'Come on now, Heathcliff,' May said, because she'd been in there when Libby had been *really* ranting...

'What *was* she going on about?' he asked. 'Heathcliff's horrible; he's abusive. God—'

'No, no, no...' May tutted. 'Lord help me!' She took another breath. This was the woman who could deal with anything and who was rarely lost for words, Alistair found himself thinking. 'I don't think Libby finds Heathcliff to be so terrible,' she said. 'You have a logical brain, Alistair. Libby does not...'

'I know.' He nodded, and despite the seriousness of what had happened he couldn't help but smile when he thought of the time they'd shared together. But then the smile faded. 'She broke things off. We weren't seeing each other for long, but...'

Like a dam ready to burst, all that he'd

held inside him since the break-up just had to come out.

'I even wrote to her—well, it was a card with my number on it, in case she'd deleted it and changed her mind, but I heard nothing back.'

'You didn't think to call her?'

'No, because I'd deleted *her* number.' He smiled wryly. 'I was so cross when she ended it. I just wiped her number straight away.'

'In case you drunk-dialled her?' May asked. 'Isn't that what you all call it now?'

'No.' He stared back. 'I don't do that kind of thing.'

'Hmmm…' May said, as if she didn't believe him. 'Now, she asked where you were and I said I'd come and get you. But remember, Alistair, Libby's not herself. She's improving, but she's still argumentative and is being quite confrontational at the moment.'

'I'm not going to upset her,' Alistair said, but then he nodded, because he had given her a bit of a smart answer before, when she'd taunted him about going out on a date with someone else. 'I understand.'

'She needs to rest—and I mean that. I'll be asking all her visitors to bear that in mind,' May said, standing to take him around to the observation ward. 'I'll take you through. But her parents should be here soon.'

'Why does that sound like a warning?'

'Oh, I'm saying nothing,' May told him. 'I'm not getting involved in this.'

Alistair thanked Brendan and Lina for staying by his side, and then walked with May through to the observation ward. There were a couple of patients that Alistair could see, though the curtains were drawn around what must be Libby's bed.

May peered around them before calling for Alistair to come in. 'Here he is!' May said to her very pale patient. 'I was just telling Alistair that your parents are almost here.'

'God...'

Libby closed her eyes. That was something she really didn't need right now. Her head felt like a pulsing rock under a desert sun, as if she'd been to a really wild party, and soon she'd have to pretend to be fine to her parents.

'I'm too tired for visitors,' she said, and then looked up at Alistair. 'I don't mean you...'

She paused. That sounded awful, and needy, and also as if she didn't like her parents when she absolutely did. It was all just too much to explain.

'I mean—'

'Shh…' Alistair said. 'It's fine. Nobody's going to stay long. I'm sure they just need to see for themselves that you're okay.'

'I fell.'

'Yes.'

'And you were here, bringing a patient in?'

'Correct.' Alistair nodded. 'Do you know what day it is?'

She thought for a second. Actually, she did. It had been a week to the day since she'd made the most regrettable mistake of her life. She knew that because she'd been counting every single day and every single night.

'Thursday.'

'Yes. And do you know who the Prime Minister is?'

'Yes,' Libby lied.

She didn't have a clue. It was scary to know you weren't thinking properly. That there were big gaps in your thinking and your memory.

'An hour?' she checked. 'I lost an hour? I still don't feel right…'

'Libby, stop panicking.' Alistair was firm.

'But I feel all foggy.'

'You are so much better than you were. Every minute you're getting better.'

'Am I?'

'Yes.'

He smiled a very nice smile and she looked at the stubble on his jaw and remembered wanting to touch it. She tried to do so now, but he caught her hand before it got there, saving her from making a complete fool of herself. Libby knew he wouldn't be here if he hadn't been passing by, but somehow she had to keep that fact in a brain that didn't seem able to hold on to anything much at the moment.

'I am sorry about all this,' she said.

'Don't be,' Alistair said, and took a seat by the bed.

'I've got concussion, apparently. Nothing exciting at all. I've got to stay in overnight and then hopefully my confusion… I don't think I'm confused now.'

'Good,' Alistair said.

'But how did you find out I was here?'

Alistair told her yet again that he'd been bringing in a patient, only this time he could see it was sinking in.

'I'm sorry if I overshared,' she said.

'You mainly spoke gibberish about how if your name was Cathy—'

'Cathy?'

'Yes, and you talked about your pelican phobia.'

'I don't have a pelican phobia…'

'You said you did,' Alistair said, omitting to add that she'd also talked about hating his new job. And his bike. And said that she had been going on a date with someone new who didn't have a bike or a dangerous job.

He would have loved nothing more than to confront her with this information, but he'd only found out about her date by accident, so he chose to ignore it, even if it hurt. Even if it really hurt that she'd broken up with him over his job.

It had already cost him his family after all.

Well, not completely. But things were still very strained. He couldn't quite believe she'd let something so good go over his work, but he was too drained to think about it now. Just exhausted with relief.

'I might go and get a coffee and then—' He cut himself off as he heard May arriving with Libby's parents. She hadn't been exaggerating when she'd told Libby they were almost here.

Her mother was tiny, with huge mascara streaks on her face, and she was so loud!

'Oh, Libby!' she choked out, and then broke into noisy sobs.

Alistair was able to witness the exact effect her mother had on Libby, because her pulse shot up and as the blood pressure cuff was released it rang out a little alarm. And no wonder.

Libby's mother stood sobbing on her husband as if their daughter lay dead in the bed.

'Mum,' Libby pleaded, 'it's just a concussion.'

'You had to be *sedated*!' she wailed. 'For a *CT*! We had to give consent!'

'Mum, please…'

Libby, Alistair noted, was actually the practical one.

'I signed my own consent form,' she told her mother. 'I do remember that!'

'I was so distressed that I had to get your father to pull over onto the emergency lane when they informed us!'

Libby's dad seemed very used to it all, and he patted his wife's shoulder with one hand while he shook Alistair's hand with the other. Brief introductions were made.

'A friend?' he checked. 'So you're not the paramedic who brought her in?'

'No.'

'Well, thanks for hanging around,' he said, rather curtly. 'We can take it from here.'

'Dad…' Libby warned, and Alistair watched as he turned to his daughter.

'Are you okay, darling?'

'Yes,' Libby said. 'And I'm sorry.'

Her father sat on the bed and took her hand, letting out a relieved sigh that Alistair completely understood—because that was what he kept doing. Every time she opened her green eyes and spoke more like the Libby he knew he wanted to sigh in relief, or let out an odd kind of half-laugh.

The same laugh that was bubbling out from her father right now—pure relief that she was fine. 'Are you sure you're okay?' he asked.

'Honestly. I'm just a bit foggy on details,' Libby said. 'And very, very tired.'

'I *knew* this would happen,' said Mrs Bennett. 'I knew that if you moved to London—'

'Come on now, Helen,' Mr Bennett said. 'London's not to blame for Libby tripping. She's always tripping.'

'I wasn't taking *drugs*!' Libby shouted. 'Why do you assume—?'

Alistair saw her father startle as his lovely Libby not only missed his meaning but also raised her voice.

'Libby!' Mr Bennett warned, and Alistair cut in.

'Your father meant falling, Libby,' he said gently, and he shot a look at her father that told Mr Bennett to remember that Libby wasn't herself.

'That's right. I meant falling,' Mr Bennett said, and then added, 'I'll bet she was wearing those heels…'

* * *

'It wasn't the heels,' Libby said, because it absolutely hadn't been her strappy sandals that had made her fall. At least, she thought not. In truth, Libby didn't actually know *what* had made her trip and fall. 'I can't remember…'

'That doesn't matter,' Alistair said.

'It does to me.' How she hated all these gaps! 'Anyway, I'm going home tomorrow,' Libby said. 'Probably…'

'We'll be right here with you until you do,' Mrs Bennett chimed in, looking around for a chair as if preparing to begin a bedside vigil.

'Helen…' Mr Bennett chided. 'She's not critically ill. We're going to a hotel and then we'll find out what's happening in the morning.'

But Helen Bennett had other ideas. 'We can stay at her flat.'

'No!' Libby said hurriedly.

Alistair watched as Libby reeled back in horror, and he couldn't help but wonder what she might have left lying around in the flat that had so recently played host to their four-day sex-fest. She was burning in a blush, so he stepped in to ease her mind.

'Libby lost her keys when she fell.' Alistair rarely lied, but he thought he should make an exception, for Libby's sake. 'I think the paramedics might have located them, but it'll take a while to get them back.'

Her green eyes met his and he saw her rapid blink of relief. But then she frowned... *'All* my keys?'

'Don't worry, we'll get it sorted,' Alistair said.

Mrs Bennett came to a decision. 'We'll go to a hotel tonight, or for as long as you're staying in hospital, but once they discharge you you're coming back with us. The doctor said you'll be off for at least two weeks and—'

'Mum, can you please *stop*?'

'Libby!' her father warned.

'Now!' May interjected. She could clearly see the blood-pressure-raising effect the visitors were having on her patient. 'I'm going to borrow your parents for a couple of moments, Libby, to go over some details.'

Alistair knew May would explain things again to her parents. He wished they had been there and seen Libby when she had first come in. Not to upset them, more so they could know just how ill she had been and how much better she was now.

Libby just lay there, pressing her fingers into her eyes.

'Oh, my God,' Libby said thankfully, as May steered her parents away—no doubt to gently remind them that their daughter wasn't quite herself right now. 'She does this all the time. She has to turn everything into a drama.'

'Really?'

'Well, not always…' Libby sighed, removing her fingers and turning her teary eyes to him. 'But she's exhausting, isn't she?'

'She's you!' Alistair smiled.

'Me?'

'Completely.' He nodded. 'Although luckily I don't—'

He stopped himself from making a light joke about not fancying her mother. It was hard to remember that there was no longer a 'them'. That they weren't together. He hadn't been called as her emergency contact; he had just happened to be here. Thankfully Libby didn't notice his brief dilemma, because she was busy with one of her own.

'Now I've upset them…' she said.

'Libby…' He was firm. 'They're the ones who should not be upsetting *you*, okay?'

'I know.' She looked up at him. 'They lost my brother before they had me.'

'I'm sorry.'

'They'd bubble wrap me if they could.'

Right now, so too would he, Alistair thought.

'*Have* I lost my keys?' Libby asked him.

'No. At least I don't think so. May put your

bag in her locker rather than the safe, so you could get access to it more easily.'

'That was nice of her.'

He so badly wanted to take her hand, but while it had felt right to do so before, when she'd been lost and struggling, it didn't feel right to do so now.

Although it felt necessary.

It felt as if it should be the most natural thing to do.

Yet she had broken them…she had undone them…and he had to remember that.

And Libby wasn't herself—he had to remember that too—so he resisted what was necessary and natural and didn't take her hand.

Then he heard her parents returning.

'I'm going to go,' Alistair said. 'I'm so pleased you're okay.'

'Thank you for everything tonight.'

'Get some rest,' Alistair said, and turned to leave.

'Alistair?'

He stood with his back to her for a second too long, and then turned. 'Yes?'

'I'm sorry for breaking us up. I made a dreadful mistake.'

'Libby, you are to rest and not get upset, so don't think about all that stuff.'

'But it's all I can think about.'

'Well, stop.'

'Will you come and see me tomorrow?'

'Get some sleep.'

That was the most important thing right now. It had to be.

Everything else could wait.

CHAPTER FIVE

ALISTAIR CAME TO see her the next day, after she had been transferred to the Neuro ward.

He was doing an extra shift, he explained when he came to visit, still wearing his uniform. 'How are you feeling?' he asked.

'Tired,' Libby admitted. 'Though that's probably because I've been woken up through the night for obs...'

'Or you could be tired because you've had a nasty fall.'

'Yes, maybe...'

She was starting to accept it, and really it was impossible not to, because as well as her head, the left side of her back and her left shoulder were tender, and on top of all that...

'I cried this morning because I didn't have a spoon on my breakfast tray. Unfortunately it coincided with the arrival of the consultant, so now they're keeping me in for an extra night.

It's normal to be overly emotional after a fall, apparently, which isn't great when you're—'

'Already overly emotional?' Alistair suggested with a smile.

Libby gave a glum nod.

'Here.' He put a bar of hazelnut chocolate— the same as the one she *hadn't* chosen the night of the fridge saga—onto the hospital bed table.

'Thank you!' She pounced and opened it immediately. 'I keep trying to explain to them that my blood pressure's only up when my mother's here.'

'Libby, it's good they're here. And you're sounding better.'

She knew she wasn't looking it, though— her bruises were really starting to come out.

'Mum and Dad keep asking for the key to my flat. I've got my bag back, with the keys in it, but I haven't told them that.'

'What *is* the problem with your flat?'

'I just don't want them poking their noses in. There are tissues everywhere from my crying over you...'

He said nothing.

'And as well as that,' Libby further explained, as she broke off another piece of chocolate, 'I saved the empty box from our condoms.'

'Why would you do that?'

'Because I didn't have anything else from us that I could keep.'

He rolled his eyes, clearly unimpressed with her version of sentimentality, and then carried on being his practical self. 'I think it's wise that they're keeping you in for another night. Libby, you really were unwell yesterday.'

'I know.'

'I'm not sure that you do.'

'I do know. And thank you for staying with me when I was so confused.' She looked up at Alistair. He had put up with so much, and yet she desperately needed one thing more. 'Alistair, I know you're going to say no, but can I ask a favour?'

'No.'

Libby chose to ignore his response and forged on. 'Would you please say that you're going to look after me for a couple of days after I'm discharged?'

'In your tiny studio flat?'

'Yes.'

'And what do I say to your father about how long I've known you?'

'Say we're just friends…new friends. Please?'

'No.' He shook his head. 'I'm not prepared to do that. I will, however, go to your flat and get a change of clothes for you, and get rid of any damning evidence, if that helps.'

It wasn't the answer Libby had wanted, but it did help the situation, so she nodded and gingerly sat up as he went over to her bedside locker and pulled out her vast boho-style bag.

'What on earth have you got in here?' Alistair asked, because it weighed a ton.

'Everything,' she said. 'If I had lost this yesterday, I'd have died.'

'It's too soon for jokes, Libby,' he warned, but then seemed to check himself.

She looked up, hearing the strain of his voice, but he looked away, so she got back to wading through the previous tenants' mail, and her make-up bag and purse, and even pulled out her missing umbrella, before finally finding her keys.

'I've put red nail varnish on the one for the flat,' Libby informed him as she handed them over.

It was just as well that she had. For the occupier of such a small studio flat, Libby had the amount of keys of a prison warden, Alistair thought, taking the jangling bunch and finding himself wanting to know why she had so many.

He hadn't asked.

He was refusing to fall back under her spell.

Or rather refusing to let her know that he hadn't yet managed to escape it.

He wanted to guard himself from her.

It was odd, because he knew her parents were nice people, but yesterday he'd wanted them to take a step back and give her space and peace. He knew they were trying, because even he had struggled to deal with Libby's rollercoaster temper, lack of filter, and melodramatic emotional state.

Alistair was usually very controlled with his feelings. His emotions were his own and it felt even more imperative now that he keep it that way.

Even if she ran riot in his head.

The relief from yesterday was still there, but now the hurt was returning, and with it a quiet anger at just how readily she'd tossed away something so good.

They *had* been good, he thought as he located the red nail varnished key and let himself into her flat.

He felt as if it should be sealed off with tape—as if he were entering the scene of a crime.

Her flat was actually very tidy.

The sofa-bed was back to being a sofa, and there was a table beside it with lots of little balls of tissues. While he believed she'd cried, Alistair did not believe that it had been over him.

Not for a second.

There were a couple of chocolate wrappers too, and little balls of foil, but he doubted they were evidence of a broken heart. She'd brought chocolate the night they'd met, after all.

The box of condoms had been turned into a bookmark. He put her dog-eared copy of *Wuthering Heights* into her bedside drawer, with the 'bookmark' in place. If her parents snooped in there then it was their own damned fault what they found.

He tried to find some sensible shoes, but it would seem she didn't possess any. There wasn't even a pair of trainers. The only flat shoes he could find were her nursing ones, so he collected them, as well as some jeans, and a few other bits she might need. He practically closed his eyes as he rummaged in her underwear drawer.

God, it killed him being her ex…

He dropped the bag of clothes and toiletries back at the hospital late in the evening, long after visiting hours.

Libby looked worse than she had that morning. There were dark rings under her eyes and her lips were pale. She was lying on the bed with no television on or anything, just dozing—but then she opened her eyes and smiled right at him, and relief came flooding back.

He wanted to do the same sighing thing that

her father had. Instead, he settled for a nod and, 'Hello.'

'Hi.' She pulled herself to sit up. 'Thanks for this.'

'I couldn't find your trainers.'

'I don't have any,' Libby said.

'But I thought you were into fitness...what with the exercise ball and yoga mat...?'

'Oh, please!' Libby waved all mention of them away. 'I keep meaning to start yoga, and I was about to deflate the exercise ball and get a chair. I read that it was good for posture, but I hate the thing.'

'Are you still being discharged tomorrow?'

'Yes. Well, they'll decide for certain in the morning, but for now it looks like I'm headed home with Mum and Dad. I'm to come back for an outpatient appointment in two weeks.'

It was too soon for her to go home, Alistair thought. He was arrogant enough to believe he was right and the consultant was wrong. It was also too soon for a two-hour drive and the raining down of questions and overbearing concern from her mother.

He had given her dilemma some thought, because even though he was cross, he still cared about her. And she really was alone in London.

'Look, it's not ideal, but you can tell them that you're coming back to mine.'

'No.' Libby shook her head, assuming he meant that she should lie to her parents and to the hospital in telling them that she'd be recovering at his place. 'It's kind of you to offer, but my mother calls all the time and she'll realise that I'm at my flat, given they helped me move in.'

'I meant,' Alistair corrected, 'that you can stay at mine, if you want.'

Libby's eyes widened in surprise. Oh, she desperately wanted to say yes, but...

'I wouldn't do that to you...'

It was hardly fair to land herself on him, given all that had passed between them, so she cast about in her bruised and shaken mind for a plausible reason to turn down his kind, albeit reluctant, offer.

'Anyway, I want to be around my own things. Please, will you just tell them you're staying with me?'

'Fine.'

And even though she could hear his supreme reluctance, Libby was simply relieved. Just so relieved that she would be able to rest and heal in peace without her mother watching her sleep, or peering in at her every five minutes.

Her father was less than impressed when she

told him her plans on the morning of her discharge; her mother was appalled.

'Libby, you barely know him.'

'I do.' She closed her eyes, but her voice was adamant. 'Alistair's coming to collect me.'

Her parents were draining…and being in hospital itself was actually exhausting.

She'd had another mainly sleepless night.

But happily there had been a spoon with her cornflakes this morning, and all her obs were behaving; she'd even had a shower with a grad nurse hovering outside in case she felt unwell. She'd been fine. Ish… And so, when the consultant came around, it was agreed that she could go home.

Phew.

Getting dressed proved a little tricky. Alistair had chosen the ugliest pair of knickers in her drawer, and of all things a strapless bra! He'd brought jeans that were too tight after so many takeaways, and there was a formal shirt she wore for interviews and such. It took a lot of effort to do up the buttons. He'd also brought her nursing shoes for her to wear. She looked quite a sight once she'd managed to put it all on.

When her parents had checked out of their hotel, they came onto the ward to collect her, they now had to say their reluctant goodbyes. Libby was sitting on her bed, waiting for her outpatient appointment and her doctor's letter, and holding her head injury information leaflet. As soon as Alistair arrived and she had her documentation she would be able to go home.

'Where's this young man, then?' her dad asked.

'He's thirty-three,' Libby snapped. 'And he's very, very responsible.'

Apart from his motorbike and his choice of career.

Hopefully he wouldn't arrive with a crash helmet for her to squeeze on, but it didn't actually matter. She had her phone and would call a cab; she just needed him to sign her out of here.

And then, finally, there he was, wearing dark jeans and a black linen shirt and carrying her coat.

'At last,' snapped Mr Bennett.

'I was just getting some shopping in,' Alistair responded—with the patience of a saint, Libby thought. 'I thought it better to get organised now, rather than leave her alone once we get back to the flat.'

Her father gave an extremely reluctant nod.

'How are you today?' Alistair smiled his professional smile at Libby.

'Better. I'm just waiting for my outpatient appointment,' she said. 'And Mum and Dad are just about to go.'

Helen didn't want to leave, though. 'We'll wait until you're discharged.'

'Dad's working tonight,' Libby said. 'Please, stop making so much fuss.' She felt wretched and so on show, with her parents carrying on as if she were ten or even twenty years younger.

They were lovely, but complicated, and she was too tired for it all right now.

'Take care, Libby,' her father said, and she could tell he was more worried about leaving her than he had been when he'd arrived.

Oh, that was so unfair, when Alistair was beyond dependable. And, yes, she had only known him a short while—she could not lie— but he was a good guy and he didn't deserve suspicious looks.

Her father pulled Alistair aside and the two of them talked quietly. Libby cringed, sure her father was lecturing Alistair.

'I love you, darling,' Mrs Bennett said. 'I'll call you tonight.'

'I'll call *you*, Mum,' Libby said. 'Don't forget, I'm going to be sleeping a lot.'

'Fine!' she snapped tartly, and looked over to Alistair as if he was somehow causing this, rather than doing his best to fix things for her.

'I'm so sorry,' Libby said once they'd gone. 'They are actually lovely.'

'I can see that they are. They don't know me, and of course they're worried about you.'

'Yes.' Libby took a breath. 'We usually get on so well, but honestly…'

'I get it.' He took a seat by the bed she still sat on. 'You're lucky they care so much. I barely talk to my parents.'

'Really?'

'Their choice,' Alistair said.

'Why?' Libby asked.

'I don't want to discuss it.'

He drew such a firm line, closed down the conversation so completely, that Libby had no choice but to accept it.

She tried to make light of his rejection. 'I'd probably forget it even if you did discuss it…' she joked. 'Honestly, my head is like a sieve. I'm sure I'd missing some vital point or say the wrong thing…'

He gave a pale smile.

'I'm sorry you're not talking with your family.'

He nodded, but refused to be drawn.

'Do you have brothers or sisters?'

'Libby, why don't you lie down?'

'Because then they might keep me in,' Libby muttered. 'I just want to go home to my own bed and to sleep into next week.'

She forced a smile at the approaching nurse.

'I've got your appointment,' the nurse said, and then turned to Alistair. 'You're going to be taking care of her?'

'Yes.'

'Then I'll go through the head injury instructions with you.'

'He's a paramedic,' Libby snapped.

But Alistair ignored her. In fact, he said something that made the nurse smile, and then listened intently as she went through all the instructions with him as if he were five years old.

It made Libby grumbly, and she didn't quite know why. 'I bet you even watch flight attendants doing their demonstration,' Libby said as they walked down a very, very long corridor. 'Just to be polite.'

'Of course I watch,' Alistair said. 'And not just to be polite—every plane is different.' As she slowed her pace he glanced over at her. 'Are you okay?'

'I'm just tired.'

They had a little rest mid-corridor, and then he put an arm around her and led her the rest of the way to the end. They came to the ambulance bay where ambulances were lined up, waiting to offload their patients.

'They're waving to you,' Libby said.

Alistair ignored them and sorted out their taxi back to her flat.

Of course he matched the registration before getting in.

The world felt a little too fractured and the radio in the car too loud. Everything seemed somehow amplified. For the first time Libby felt a flutter of panic as to how she was going to manage, and questioned her decision to wave her parents off and send them home.

'Oh!' she said as they arrived inside her front door—because he hadn't just picked up her coat and clothes, he had also cleaned! The flat was gleaming, and when she opened her lovely fridge she saw that he really had been shopping for her. 'That's so kind. I really do appreciate it. I'll transfer the money...'

'It's fine. I'll be eating a lot of it.'

'Don't be daft. I don't expect you to *actually* take care of me. Just call, or pop in whenever. But really—'

'I'm not leaving you—at least for the first few days,' he said. 'The instructions are very clear.'

'Yes, but I've got one tiny sofa-bed.'

'And I shan't be getting into it,' he said.

'Where are you going to sit?'

On her exercise ball. That was apparently his plan. And later, when she woke from a doze and saw him stretched out on her yoga mat on the floor, she couldn't believe it.

He turned his head and looked at her. 'How do you feel?'

'Worse than I did at the hospital.'

'They said you'd feel like that. Have some water and try and go back to sleep.'

He was being lovely, but really she felt so dreadful that had she been on her own she'd have been scared.

Later still... 'I feel a bit nauseous,' she admitted.

'There's a bowl there if you have to vomit.'

And even later... 'I've got a really, really bad headache.'

'Because you've got a really, really big bruise. Would you like two headache tablets?'

Two headache tablets aren't going to fix this, Libby grumbled to herself.

But she took them anyway, and then suddenly it was dark outside. She realised she must have been asleep and the tablets might just have worked!

'What time is it?'

'Six,' Alistair said. 'I'll get you something to eat, shall I?'

'I'm not hungry.'

'Just something light?' he suggested. 'Why don't you call your parents?'

'I guess...' She sat up in bed and went through her bag for a comb. After she'd attacked her hair, she tried to look suitably bright as she reassured her mother on a video call for five minutes. And then she held the phone for her father, and Alistair gave him a wave from where he was sitting on her exercise ball.

'Don't worry,' Alistair said. 'I'm keeping a close eye.'

And he was.

'You can lie here,' Libby said, when she'd changed into fresh pyjamas and saw he was flicking out a sleeping bag onto her yoga mat.

'No,' he told her. 'You dumped me; you don't get to share a bed with me.'

'I didn't dump you,' Libby attempted. 'We fizzled out.'

'No, we didn't. And that's hardly an invitation to bed.'

There was very little dignity in her scrambled brain. 'I know we didn't fizzle out—well, I know it didn't fizzle out for me. I've missed you so very much…'

He gave her a tight, mirthless smile. 'Get some rest.'

'Alistair…'

'Libby, you need to rest.'

It was hard to rest, though, with him beside her. Admittedly, she felt better able to rest with him beside her than she would have at her family home or if she were alone, but…

'Alistair?'

'Go to sleep, Libby, or just lie quietly and relax. We are not getting into this.'

Not now, and nor the next day, apparently, because when she awoke Alistair was talking on his phone, and then he came out from her tiny kitchen and it seemed a decision had been made.

'You'll have to come to mine,' Alistair told her. 'I've got a spare room.'

'I really don't need taking care of...'

'You need to be watched,' Alistair said. 'And you need to rest or you could run into problems. Please take this seriously, Libby. I've already lost one friend because he chose not to follow medical advice.'

'I am taking this seriously,' Libby said. 'That's why I didn't want to go back to my parents'. I haven't lived at home since I was eighteen. And I know I need to be quiet and rest.'

'Then you also know you shouldn't be on your own. And I don't want to sleep on a yoga mat or sit on your exercise ball. If I've got to be stuck with you, then I'd at least like a little space and comfort.'

'Stuck?'

'Yes,' Alistair said. 'I landed myself in it, so I'm not blaming you, but I'm pretty much stuck with you for the next few days. Unless you want to call your parents to come and collect you, or unless you have a friend who doesn't mind dropping everything and coming here to stay.'

'Stuck?' she checked again, inviting him to change his choice of word, but he nodded. 'You're not a very nice nurse.'

'I'm not,' he agreed. 'And right now you're not a very nice patient. But that's because you're not yet yourself.'

'I am.'

'No,' he said, 'you are not. You're being a right little madam, in fact.' He looked directly at her. 'I'll pack a few things for you.'

'I need—'

'Libby, I do this all the time when I'm taking a patient into hospital. Phone, charger, laptop, charger, knickers, pyjamas, toothbrush, hairbrush or comb, shampoo, deodorant, tampons, pads... Any medication?'

'No.'

Good grief, he was efficient.

In mere minutes he had achieved what would have taken her an entire morning—and even then she'd have left something behind.

'Moisturiser,' Libby said as he came out of her bathroom.

'I've got it,' he said. 'I'll just take the perishables out of your fridge...'

'How long am I coming to yours for?'

'I'm not your doctor, Libby. How long would you have stayed at home? How long until you'd have been ready to take the train back down to London and get on the underground? Go shopping and look after your flat?'

'I am sorry,' she said. 'I wasn't really thinking straight when I suggested this.'

'No,' he said, 'but I was, and I agreed to it, so blame me if you want. Come on.'

It was a very bright winter morning, and everything was wet. The glare was a lot for her to take, so she sat on the wall with her eyes closed as they waited for a cab.

'You make me feel so incompetent.'

'I don't intend to; I'm trying to be practical,' he said, and sat on the wall beside her. 'And you're certainly not incompetent.'

She wasn't, Alistair knew, for she had very competently captured his very controlled heart.

Then tossed it away.

Then taken it back.

He was not going to get into a row with her now—of course not. But at the same time he was not going to let himself get drawn into this, or let her flirt with him.

She was still a bit… Not confused, but it was more she was just not quite herself. She was cross, teary, and still unaware of just how un-well she had been and how much time it would take her to heal.

He turned and looked at her, sitting on the wall with her eyes closed, and he felt that odd little sigh again.

His mouth closed into a grim line.

Her anger seemed to be fading.

Just as his was returning.

Libby definitely wasn't feeling herself, because she slept in the car. And she must trust him im-plicitly, because she didn't know the street he lived in—just that the front door of his house was cobalt blue, there was a pot of earth beside it and that it said number thirty-five.

'If you collapse,' Libby said, 'and I have to call an ambulance, I shan't know your address…'

'You can use the co-ordinates on your phone,' he said as he opened up the front door, but then he told her where she was.

'I'm none the wiser,' Libby said, because she really didn't know London at all.

'Come in.'

There was a staircase to one side of the hall, which was long and led to a kitchen.

'The lounge is through here,' Alistair said.

She peered in and glimpsed a large leather

sofa and a chair by a fireplace, but then they carried on down the hall to the kitchen. It was small, but bright and modern, with large French doors that led out into a narrow garden. There was a high breakfast bar, and a kitchen table with pretty pot plants in quirky containers.

The washing machine was in the kitchen, and humming away—which confused her, because he'd been at her flat all night.

'Is there a delay button on that?' Libby asked.

Perhaps it was odd to be trying to make sense of his washing matching, when she wasn't quite sure of the month or who the Prime Minister was, but she couldn't stop fixating on it.

'Don't worry about that now,' Alistair said.

Perhaps he saw how droopy she was. It felt like too much effort to pull out a chair, and the breakfast bar stools looked too high, so she just stood there, feeling a little overwhelmed.

'I'll show you the guest room.'

'How do you work and keep it so neat?' she asked as they climbed the stairs.

'I have a cleaner once a week,' Alistair said, showing her the bathroom, which was opposite the room where she would sleep. 'I asked her to come and sort out the guest room—that's why the washing machine is on.'

'Oh.'

She glanced down the hall and saw a half-open pale wooden door, which she guessed was his bedroom. Libby wanted to look behind that door so much that she tuned out of what he was saying about what Chloe, his cleaner, had bought for Libby's arrival.

'I asked her to buy sheets, a duvet and pillows, towels...'

'I'm an expensive person to be stuck with.'

'It's fine. I kept meaning to get round to buying all that anyway. The spare bed's never even been made up before.'

His cleaner had good taste, because the bed was dressed in white linen. She was thoughtful, too, because there was even a box of tissues by her bed. The room's walls were a lovely soft grey. Libby knew that if she'd risked grey walls they would have ended up looking like a prison cell. Instead they looked soft and pretty—it was a lovely guest room. She was surprised he'd never so much as made up the bed...

'Don't you have friends who stay over?'

'Libby, my overnight guests generally sleep in *my* bed.'

Ouch!

She screwed up her nose at the thought of his overnight guests and really, really hoped he wouldn't be having any while she was there.

Not that she could object, of course, but it would be torture.

As well as completely her own fault.

She sat on the edge of the pretty white bed and looked up at him, recalling how he'd invited her into his home once before, and her response had been to end things with him. She could have been in his bed, in his bedroom, but instead it was unseen and forbidden to her, hidden behind a pale wooden door.

'I'm sorry, Alistair...' There was no dignity in concussion, because she felt her face screw up and tears start tumbling out of her eyes. 'I made a mistake.'

'Please don't cry...'

'I don't usually,' Libby attempted. 'It's my head injury...'

'Libby, you were sobbing over a fridge the day we met.'

'It wasn't just the fridge I was crying about.'

'Okay...'

'The fridge was the final straw. I was having a bad day—at least I was until you showed up.'

'Okay,' he said again.

But Libby noticed that, unlike when they'd been together, he didn't ask her to elaborate, or try to find out more about her life. In fact, he was quietly and calmly putting away her things, unpacking her bag for her as she sat there, listless. She didn't mind. The contents were hardly private—he'd packed it after all.

'Why don't you try and get some rest?' he suggested, putting her pale blue pyjamas on the bed. 'Maybe get changed and get into bed and I'll bring you up some lunch.'

'Aren't I allowed downstairs?'

'Of course you are.'

She was just feeling so completely listless, though. Even the effort of relocating to his flat had depleted her.

She picked up her handbag and started to go through it.

'What are you looking for?' he asked.

'Headache tablets.'

'I'll bring you some up with your lunch,' Alistair said. 'Do you want to give me your toiletry bag and I'll put your things in the bathroom?' As she nodded he added, 'You're the white towels.'

It was such a little thing, to be the white towels, but it stung so very much.

She thought back to their time together...to Alistair with her lemon-coloured daisy towel around his hips.

Now she was relegated to newly bought guest towels.

She piled her clothes onto a chair and pulled on the pyjamas, even though they were more suitable for summer, and then padded over to the bathroom.

It was a very boldly decorated bathroom, with jade walls and towels and a huge white enamel bath that she would have loved to fill and sink into, but the doctor had warned her to avoid baths until after her outpatient appointment.

Over the bath was a shower, but she would tackle that tomorrow, Libby thought, peering at the lovely green towels that were forbidden to her.

Then she stopped sulking as she caught sight of herself in the mirror.

Gosh!

It was the first time she'd really seen herself since the accident.

There had been mirrors in the hospital bathrooms, of course, but it had taken all her mental energy just to wash her hands and dry them.

Or possibly she'd been avoiding looking at them.

Now she peered into his mirror.

The green décor could be to blame for giving her complexion such a sallow hue, but there was nothing to account for the dark shadows under her eyes.

Were they bruises?

They were so dark Libby actually considered it for a moment—but no, they were shadows.

There *were* bruises, though. Not just the one

she couldn't see, on the back of her head, one on her hand, and one inside her elbow, where they'd put in drips.

Now, she took off her pyjama top and saw that her left shoulder looked as if it had been painted purple. And it was no wonder her back hurt, because as she turned around she saw not just bruising, but the actual imprint of the lines of the escalator on her skin.

She swallowed—it really had been some fall.

Her top went back on and she made her way to the guest room, where it was actually bliss to sink into very comfortable sheets and soft pillows and hear Alistair coming up the stairs.

'Here,' Alistair said, and came in carrying a tray. 'Have some lunch.'

Libby sat up and looked at the pretty tray, all dotted with poppies, and a rather delectable-looking lunch. 'Chicken soup?'

'Good for the soul, apparently,' Alistair said. 'Mind you, it's just from a tin.'

Ahh, but it had been warmed by him, and served with lovely buttery toast, two head-ache tablets and a big jug of water with a glass, which he put by the bed.

'I'm all bruised...'

'Yes.'

'Not just the back of my head. My shoulder and back are too.'

'I saw at the hospital.' Alistair nodded.

'I feel like you know more about me than I do,' Libby admitted. 'I hate missing that hour…'

'Listen…' he held the tray steady and then sat on the bed '… I helped turn you and get you off the spinal board…'

'What did I say?' She had an awful feeling she might have told him she loved him, or something embarrassing.

'You repeated yourself a lot,' Alistair said. 'Just asking where you were…'

'What else did I say?'

He took a breath. 'Once we'd got past the pelicans, and Cathy, you said you were cross about my job…'

'Yes.' Libby nodded. She remembered that.

'And my bike.'

'Yes.' She sort of remembered that. 'What else?'

He was quiet for a moment. 'Not much.'

'Alistair?'

'You said you were going on a date…'

'No.'

'What?'

'I mean, I *was* going on a date, but I changed my mind,' she said. 'I knew I'd made a mistake.'

'Stop!' he said, gently but firmly.

'But I did.'

She could remember now, turning around, knowing she had to see Alistair, but he was refusing to be drawn into her version of events.

'I changed my mind and turned to go back down the stairs.'

She remembered that moment now. And the moments leading up to her fall. Realising she was on the wooden escalator, not stairs, the blinding veil of her tears, the realisation that she had to see Alistair—had to tell him why she had ended things and that she didn't want it to be over between them.

'I knew I had to see you.'

'Okay,' he said, and moved to stand up from the bed. 'Have your lunch.'

'You don't believe me?'

His eyes met hers. 'No,' he said. 'I don't. But I'm not going to argue about it.'

'Talk to me about it, then.'

'I don't want to talk about it, Libby. You're here because right now you need someone to take care of you, and it would seem that person is me.'

He gave her no more than that.

Yes, Alistair was taking caring of her, but on *his* terms.

Meals were brought in on the poppy tray,

and headache tablets too, and there was one awkward moment the next day when she didn't know how to turn on the hot water for the shower.

Wrapped in a white towel, she had no choice but to call out.

'Sorry...' Libby said.

'It's fine.'

He didn't give her so much as a look, just a practical lesson on the nuances of his hot water system.

'Thank you.'

He didn't respond, just headed out, closing the door behind him. 'Call if you need any-thing, or if you get dizzy.'

'Thank you.'

It wasn't even awkward to know that he was listening out for her in case she felt unwell.

It just made her feel sad.

And then irritable when she rinsed out her shampoo and couldn't find her conditioner. 'You didn't pack my conditioner,' she called. 'Can I use yours?'

'I don't have any!' he called back. 'I don't use it.'

Grumbling about dry hair and curls, she turned his odd hot water system off and wrapped herself in a guest towel. Then she sat on the edge of the bath, wondering how she could be complaining when he had done so much for her.

'Are you okay?' he called, and she guessed the silence was concerning him.

'Yes.'

'Good.'

With the water off she heard him leave his post and head down the stairs. Avoiding her, she was sure.

When she ventured downstairs a couple of evenings later, that thought was confirmed.

She was starting to feel better, more herself.

A little bored, actually!

He was sprawled on the sofa, his long legs spread along the length of it, his shirt loose and unbuttoned, exposing his chest. He was watching football on TV. His team, she knew, because in their dizzy four days of bliss he'd told her who he supported. And she'd heard him urging them on as she came down the stairs.

He glanced at her as she entered, but didn't move or make a space for her, so she sat on the chair next to the sofa.

'Good game?' she asked.

'Mmm...' He must have seen her looking at his bare chest, for he started buttoning his shirt.

A few minutes later he stretched, rose from the couch and walked towards the stairs.

She glanced at him, puzzled. 'Are you leaving?'

The game had gone into extra time and promised a nail-biting finish.

He lifted an indifferent shoulder. 'I've got some studying to do.'

'But it's going to penalties,' Libby said, not quite understanding, because even with her zero interest in sport this game was clearly an exciting one. And it was his team.

'Here.' He handed her the remote. 'I'll say goodnight. Call out if you need anything.'

'You mean you're going to bed now?'

It was early.

'I'm going up now.' His voice was flat, uninterested.

'You're not making me feel very welcome, Alistair.'

He spun back round. Eyes that had once held hers so tenderly were angry, and they refused to meet hers, but his voice was, as always, was measured and calm.

'Listen, Libby, you've got the full run of the house, an on-call paramedic, meals, a bed…' He took a deep breath. 'I'm trying to be polite here…'

She bit her lip and fought her frustration—

because this wasn't the Alistair she'd once known. 'But you're not as you were…'

'You didn't particularly like that version of me either, did you?' he reminded her. 'Now, I'm not arguing, and I'm not interested in discussing it. You're not supposed to be getting worked up and I'm trying to facilitate that as best I can. But smiling and pretending everything's fine…? Lying on the sofa together…?'

Oh, yes, he'd obviously seen her hovering, seen her hoping he'd make room for her.

He shook his head as he told her, 'That I can't and won't do.'

He walked out and left her holding the remote, staring blankly at a game she had no interest in play out its final desperate minutes.

Alistair's team won.

Libby knew it was she who had lost.

CHAPTER SIX

ALISTAIR MIGHT NOT be the cheeriest nurse, but he was incredibly efficient and Libby was very well looked after.

Several days and nights passed. She slept a great deal, and each day when she woke she felt a little better.

Slowly, she was healing.

The bruises on her back and shoulder were fading, her head felt much clearer, and she wasn't so snappy or teary any more.

Or so needy.

Every day she returned a little more to herself.

And every day Alistair distanced himself just a little bit more.

The hand-holding had stopped on the night of the accident and never returned.

And now there was no sitting on her bed and reassuring her, as he had on the day she'd arrived.

Alistair provided her with meals that tempted her appetite. He was taking good care of her, even if he hardly talked and barely looked at her. And when he did it was in a distant, almost professional way.

He was treating her as if she was his patient.

Not his lover.

Nor even his friend.

And the distance he placed between them reminded her of everything that might have been and all that she had lost.

She'd made such a mess of things, but she couldn't turn back the clock. She just had to live with the now and hope it would get better.

And even though he was cross—she knew that he was—Alistair was still a very soothing person to be around. So much so that each time she woke up she mentally located him. It was as if her heart had to know whether he was downstairs, or in his room, or in the bathroom.

He worked hard, even on his days off. She heard him listening to lectures, or tapping away on his computer. Sometimes she caught the low-pitched murmur of his voice on the phone, and tried not to wonder who he was talking to.

It was none of her business. He'd made that more than clear.

She was coming to know the sounds of the house and his routines. Each morning she heard the creak of the central heating that he only ever put on after he woke in the morning. Why didn't he set a timer?

This morning it was cold, and she heard his bare feet padding on the floorboards as he passed her room. He muttered something, cursing the bitter morning as he ran downstairs.

Did he sleep naked? It was her first one of *those* thoughts. She closed her eyes and tried not to imagine him sprinting down to the kettle, naked, his long legs taking the stairs two at a time, his strong, lean body once warm from his bed now shivering in the cold air.

But no, he wouldn't. She was his guest—an unwanted guest at that—and he wouldn't risk them bumping into each other on the landing. More was the pity!

She lay there, straining her ears to hear who he was speaking to on the phone and wishing he'd packed conditioner. Or lip balm. Or anything for her flirting arsenal. But no, she had nothing. Just her returning spirit, along with the pale blue summer pyjamas she was coming to loathe, and a second pair of ugly red tartan flannelette ones. She wore them on rotation, and handed him her washing each day, but today she was going to do it herself.

She didn't need him, Libby was sure.

'When are you back at work?' she asked,

when he knocked and came in with a breakfast of cereal, toast and a mug of tea.

'Not for a couple more days. I've swapped some shifts around. How are you feeling?'

'A lot better,' Libby said.

'Good.'

'I think I can go home.'

'To your parents'?'

'No.' She shook her head. 'Back to my flat.'

'Okay,' Alistair said. 'When you've finished eating, take your tray down and do the dishes. Then, after your shower, your sheets will need to be changed. There's another set in the second drawer and you'll need to put the others in the washing machine.' He frowned. 'You don't have a washing machine at your place, do you? Why don't you try going to the laundromat today? It's not far, and you can use it as a trial—to see how well you can manage.'

'Of course I can manage,' she forced herself to say. That look in his eye was a challenge and she wasn't going to back down from it.

He raised a brow. 'Good. Well, in that case, on your way back you can buy some bread, cheese and lettuce—or whatever you fancy for lunch. Then, if you feel fine after all that, we'll talk about you going home.'

The prospect of all those normal daily tasks felt ridiculously daunting.

Impossibly so.

'I am joking, Libby,' he said, and she looked up. 'You're better, but...'

He'd been wonderful to her, she knew, but they couldn't go on like this.

She'd been promoted to the sofa by day, which meant he moved upstairs when she came down. It was as if he couldn't bear to be in the same room as her.

And he no longer hovered like a worried parent when she took her shower.

'I'll call my parents,' Libby said wearily. 'I really shouldn't have landed all this on you. I just wasn't thinking things through.'

'Of course you weren't. You were ill.'

'Even so, I didn't realise I'd be such a...' she cast around for the right word '...such a responsibility.' And he was so...well, *responsible*. 'I don't need a full-time carer now. Just...'

She sighed, thinking of her old bedroom and the drama of her mother, compared with the lovely soft grey walls and the sheer bliss of being with Alistair, even if he was being distant.

Even if he didn't like her any more.

His eyes still refused to meet hers.

'I spoke to Dad last night,' Libby said. 'I think he's off today. He could drive down...'

'Listen.' Alistair sounded practical. 'I'm going out for lunch, to give us both some space, and then if you're up to it we can go for a walk this afternoon.'

'A walk?'

'Just along the canal,' he said. 'Then tomorrow I've got a few things on, and we'll see how you are. After that I'm back at work—two day shifts and two nights—and by then you should be fine to go back to your flat. If not, you'll have to go to your parents' as I'll be on my course.'

'I'm taking up so much of your time…'

'Not really. I've got loads of studying done— I had to do it before the residential, so being housebound has had some advantages.'

'When do you leave?' Libby asked.

'At the end of the week. I've just got that one more block of shifts before I go.'

'You've taken time off, haven't you?'

'It's fine,' he said.

'I didn't want you to use up your leave on me.'

'I was going to have a week off before I left for the course, to do all the studying. I just moved things around and am having it now.'

'Hardly a holiday…' Libby sighed. 'Is Brendan still pushing for you to have leaving drinks?'

'A few of us are getting together, yes.'

There was a stretch of silence, but no invitation for her to join them. Of course not. Libby knew she had seen to that herself.

'Thank you for taking such good care of me. And I do mean that. It's far more than I deserve—'

He threw up a hand. 'Of course you deserve to be taken care of. Let's just get you well and then you can go home.'

His brisk, practical attitude showed Libby he was done with her drama—done with *them*— and as he left her to have her breakfast it was quite a feat to give him a polite thank-you and not give in to the distress that swamped her.

So hard to be in the house with the person she possibly loved. And so hard to face up to the fact—which he'd made more than clear— that he no longer wanted her.

She took a shower and came back to fresh sheets—he'd changed them for her. She sighed.

Libby decided the sofa could wait until he went out. She knew he'd only head upstairs if she went down, so she tried to give him the space he clearly needed.

She must have fallen asleep, because she woke to the stunning sight of Alistair in a dark suit with a white shirt and sliver-grey tie, freshly shaven and carrying her tray. Well, *his* tray—but it felt like hers now. On it was a cheese, pickle and lettuce sandwich, a packet of crisps, a mug of tea and two chocolate biscuits. He told her they were for later, as he was going out.

He was perfect…so perfect.

Except for the polite, distant smile.

'You look lovely,' Libby said, and then swallowed when he didn't respond. 'Sorry. I didn't realise I wasn't allowed to make personal observations.'

He almost—*almost*—smiled. 'I'm heading off. Text me if you need anything.'

'I will,' she lied, rather than tell him she no longer had his number. But he halted at the bedroom door and then turned around.

'Have you still got my number, Libby?'

She avoided his eyes. 'I'll be fine.'

There was no *almost* smile now. 'So you deleted it, then?'

She closed her eyes in shame as she nodded, then opened them to the sight of Alistair by the bedside table, taking out a pen and writing his number down. He was so close that she had to fight not to reach out for him.

'I was scared I'd give in and call you…'

'What? You mean you'd have called when you fancied a shag?'

It was his first display of bitterness and his

cynical words cut into her. It had never been like that, but she wouldn't be able to convince him now.

'No! I ended things because I was upset about your job—'

He cut her off. 'You don't have to explain, Libby. I'm more than used to it. I'm going to lunch with my father. He too dumped me when I changed careers.' He gave her no time to ask for more on the subject. 'Call me if you need me,' he said, and then he was gone.

She had hurt him so very much, Libby knew. And he point-blank refused to talk about it.

When he got back from his lunch he didn't come up to see her.

'How are you?' he called up the stairs.

'Fine, thank you.'

There would be no gentle walk by the canal today.

CHAPTER SEVEN

SHE WOKE TO a reminder about her gynae appointment and called to reschedule. She dug in her bag for a pen. There she found the bundle of post that belonged to the previous occupant of her flat.

Not at this address, Libby wrote. *Not at this address... Not at this address...*

Even writing one phrase over and over was exhausting, but just as she was about to give up on the task she stilled, because there was a pale lilac envelope and it was addressed to her.

Oh! It was a sympathy card.

Thinking of you, it said on the front. And inside it said, *Wishing I could be there.*

Alistair.

He'd signed his name and beneath was a phone number. She checked it against the one he had written down by the bedside. It was his.

He came in then.

'Alistair…' She looked up. 'Why did you send me a sympathy card?'

'I didn't.'

'Yes, you did. It says, *"Thinking of you"*. And inside it says *"Wishing I could be there"*, and it has purple flowers on it. It's a sympathy card.'

'No,' he said. 'It's just…' He took the card and looked at it. 'I thought it was just a *thinking of you* card,' he said, blushing. 'Is this honestly a sympathy card?'

'Yes!' She smiled a watery smile.

'You must have thought I was a right jerk…'

'I've only just seen it. I've been getting the old tenant's mail and I haven't gone through it all yet. When did you send it?'

He shrugged, but didn't answer.

'I think it's lovely. And I'd have thought the same if I'd got it before. I'd have caved if I hadn't deleted your number. Actually, I was already caving. I was going to plead for help at the phone shop, to see if they could retrieve it…' She paused. 'You don't believe me?'

'I don't,' he stated, but without malice. 'I sent it a couple of days after you broke things off. I was on a night shift, getting petrol and buying a coffee…' He gave a wry smile. 'Lina asked if I was okay when she saw it. She must have thought I'd lost someone.'

* * *

Alistair thought back to that bleak night.

He *had* lost someone: Libby.

Stopping at the petrol station for a coffee, and seeing the card on a display rack by the coffee machine, he had been struck by how it stated exactly what he'd been feeling.

He'd bought the card and a stamp along with his coffee, written his number in it, and posted it before he could talk himself out of it.

Pride had kicked in since.

He was too proud for his own good, Alistair knew.

Too private, perhaps.

He didn't share his thoughts easily—unlike Libby, who had just blurted them out even before she'd had her accident.

Alistair wanted to believe her.

He wanted to believe that she'd changed her mind—that she'd missed him even a tenth as much as he'd missed her.

That she'd only just seen this card.

Only he didn't.

Oh, he believed she might regret it a bit—or was it more a case that he was now suddenly convenient?

They needed to talk. He knew that, although he had been putting it off. Because if they didn't there was the risk of falling into bed with each other again.

Not yet—but as her energy and health started to return there were moments, increasingly frequent moments of late, during which he had to ignore the memory of her body and the scent of her. Moments like now, when he had to deliberately *not* notice that the bottom button of her pyjama top was undone, and ignore the glimpse of pale stomach that he had once inhaled and deeply kissed, touched, lingered over...

Damn you, Libby Bennett.

He refused to fall in deeper, only to be spat out later, when Libby got bored again...

'Do you want to go for a walk?' he offered, because otherwise he might just move forward.

'A walk?' Libby said.

'Yes.'

For Alistair, it was a far safer bet.

Alistair gave her some sunglasses and watched as she put on her nursing shoes, jeans and one of his jumpers. Without conditioner, her curls were frizzy, and she must look such a fright.

But, even so, it was actually lovely to be out.

The canal was a very short walk from his house. It was a little frosty, though, and he suggested she take his arm—but it wasn't for any reason other than to avoid her tripping over or fainting.

'Your father said you trip a lot,' he said.

'Not a lot. But I might have to retire my heels for a few weeks.'

'You were in a summer dress and sandals when you fell.'

'I had a coat on.' She suddenly laughed. 'I probably looked like a stripper!' She saw him smile. 'It was the most stupid thing ever. I was so very determined to prove you were just a crush, and then the guy at the doughnut shop asked if I wanted to go for a drink...' She felt helpless as she tried to explain. 'I mean, how dangerous can working in a coffee shop be?'

She'd wanted safe.

And yet Alistair, even with risk attached, made her feel safer than anyone ever had.

'I can't ever go back to that café now,' she said. 'And it's a shame because they did amazing doughnuts. But—'

'You could always tell him what happened.'

'God, no. I didn't even want to go. I'd changed my mind. Like I told you, I didn't get my heel caught. I turned around because I'd changed my mind, and I forgot, just for a second, that I wasn't on the stairs—you can't go *down* an up escalator...'

He didn't believe her. She could feel it in his

silence and in the way he looked ahead as he walked.

'It's true,' Libby insisted into the silence. 'I knew I'd made a dreadful mistake. I missed you so much. And I just panicked. There had been a fatal motorbike accident the morning you left mine...'

Alistair turned and she felt his eyes on her.

'The rider didn't even make it into the department. We got stood down. For a while I thought it could be you. I knew I was overreacting, but...' She gave a hopeless shrug. 'Or perhaps I wasn't? I've hated motorbikes since I worked on an orthopaedic ward.'

'I've done advanced courses.'

'Good for you,' Libby said, a little sharply. 'And then that afternoon I heard you'd been accepted for a job that will place you right in the hot zones...'

'Yet you didn't think to talk to me about it?'

'What good was talking going to do?' she asked. 'You weren't going to change your job, or give up your bike, and I knew I had no right to ask. I didn't want you to change; it's me who has the issues.'

'Yes,' he said—but nicely. He smiled, and the arm she was leaning on felt a little more like a friend's arm than the support of a physiotherapist.

Not a lover's arm, though.

'I can't ask you not to take this job.'

'I wouldn't have given it up even if you had asked, but we could have spoken about it,' Alistair said. 'And may I point out that you're the one who's currently injured? *I'm* fine...'

'You've seen what my mother's like. I love her so much, but I swore I'd never get involved with a firefighter or anything dangerous because I've seen the toll her worrying takes on both her and my father.'

'Libby, your parents are very, very happy— well, they seem happy to me. Are you saying your mum wishes she'd never met him?'

'Of course not!'

'Your mother might worry all day if he were working in doughnut shop...'

Libby took a breath. What he was saying made perfect sense. Logical sense.

But it didn't factor in the leaping salmon in her chest that was disguised as a heart.

'It *is* a dangerous job you'll be doing, Alistair. And it scares me. Or maybe it was how much I liked you that scared me. And I had this appointment coming up, and I felt all churned up—'

'Appointment?'

'My malfunctioning ovaries.' She took a breath. 'That one *"almost serious"* relationship I told you about? He didn't take it very well when I said I was going to have some investigations.'

'He broke off with you because of that?'

'No, I broke it off with him. I was already upset, and he just made it a thousand times worse.'

'What about your parents?' Alistair asked.

'I haven't told them. Can you imagine my mother?' He didn't answer, though she didn't really pause long enough for him to respond. 'I don't know… I was just confused, because I really liked you, and I didn't want to kick things off with my fertility issues, your career path issues, motorbike issues…'

Alistair spoke then. 'Do you want a coffee?'

'Please.'

They went into a lovely café and looked at the menu. 'You've put me off doughnuts…' he said. 'Although they're really good here too.'

'Why don't we both have one and just get over our doughnut issues?' Libby suggested. 'Because I don't want to live a doughnut-free life…'

He looked at her with his lovely brown eyes. 'Custard or jam?' he asked.

'Chocolate custard, please,' Libby said. 'How about you?'

'I think I'll have chocolate custard too.'

'And I'm getting this,' Libby told him once they'd given their orders. 'No arguments.'

'There'll be no arguments from me...but you didn't bring your bag.'

Libby laughed as she glanced down at the floor and then to the chair, where she'd usually put it and saw that he was completely right. 'God, I'm a liability. If I'd been on my own I'd have ordered...' She blew out a breath. 'I am *not* this totally teary, dippy person.'

'I know that. And you're not *totally* teary and dippy,' he smiled. 'You are a lot better. I can see it.'

'I'm going to be much more empathetic when I give out head injury instructions in the future. I would never have thought it could be like this.'

'That's why your parents were worried about leaving you with a stranger and why I was never going to leave you on your own. Your father video calls me every day for updates.'

'Does he?' She closed her eyes for a moment and let out a big sigh.

'I don't blame him,' Alistair said. 'You really haven't been well.'

'I know... We are close, and they're both great when things are going well.' She gave him a tight smile. 'You know how you've spent the last few days trying not to upset me...?'

He nodded.

'Well, that's my whole life. I love my mother, but she's so easily upset. I know you said that I'm like her...' She puffed out a breath of frustration. 'He really calls you every day?'

'I try and take it downstairs, so you don't find out just how closely you're being watched.'

'I thought you were running for the kettle.'

'I've got an app for my kettle,' Alistair said. 'I can turn it on from my bed.'

Libby looked out at the glittering canal, because it was easier than looking at him and trying not to offer a flirty reply about what else he could turn on from his bed.

Perhaps the one ounce of self-restraint she possessed where Alistair was concerned was finally returning.

And so, rather than flirt, she watched the cold ducks. The drakes were looking spectacular, with their glossy plumage, all ready to dazzle the females come mating time.

'What are female ducks called?' Libby asked.

'Ducks, I think.'

She snorted. In that moment, Libby felt like a duck, drab and unimpressive, while he sat there so effortlessly gorgeous and glossy.

For a while there she'd been the luckiest duck in the world.

She just wished she hadn't stuffed things up so badly.

Or possibly it was for the best that she had?

She thought back to that dreadful morning and the fear that had clutched at her heart when the alert had come in that the motorcyclist had been killed.

She knew there were accidents all the time—though thankfully not always with such dire consequences. But then on top of that had come the news of his new job.

She had been trying to get used to the feelings he provoked in her—to the lurch in her heart, to the impact of Alistair on her life.

Such an impact...

'Yes, females are called ducks,' Alistair said, putting down his phone.

'My own personal fact-checker.' Libby smiled, but then it wavered, because she knew she didn't have him for much longer—this walk was another step closer to her going home and being out of his life, only for good this time.

'Why are you fighting with your parents?' Libby ventured.

'It's not that dramatic. We're not arguing or anything. Well, not any more.'

He stirred some more sugar into his coffee, though to her it looked as if it was more for something to do as he considered how much to reveal.

'I come a family of high achievers and my father simply could not get that I didn't want the same thing. Especially as I was enjoying working in corporate law, and the life it afforded and all that. But then my friend died and I took stock. Do you know what my father said when I told him I wanted to be a paramedic?'

'What?'

'He said, "Well, that was a waste of a good education."'

'I'm so sorry.'

'I love him. He's an arrogant prick, but I love my parents. We're at a stalemate, though. I went to lunch with him and one of his clients yesterday. I used to keep my hand in, but that's finishing up now. Once this project concludes I don't see anything to keep us seeing each other.'

'What about your mother?'

'I have coffee with her now and then, but it's tense. We don't talk about my work. We don't talk about a lot of things. I've kept my hours up—for now—because I agreed to do that when I told them I was training as a paramedic. But I know they're just waiting for me to change my mind. I haven't.' He looked over to her then, and she knew the next words were also for her. 'I won't.'

'I've never asked you to change your mind,' Libby pointed out.

'I know. You just decided someone doing my new job wasn't for you.'

'It could be...' She blinked.

Only, it was no longer just his work that was the issue.

'In a couple of days I'm going away for six weeks, and then I'll be busy in a new job.'

She had broken his trust, Libby knew.

He shook his head, then said, 'Maybe we're just not suited.'

He got up to pay and she sat there, staring into space, with tears gathering in her eyes. They left the café and walked under grey skies.

'It's started to rain,' Libby said, and was terribly grateful for it, because it meant her tears would go unnoticed.

She took his lovely arm again, all the while hating herself for all that she'd lost when she ended things with Alistair. Even if he didn't think so, she thought they were very suited. She thought he was perfect.

'It's for the best,' he said, trying to make light in the gloom as they walked along the canal. 'You'd be a nervous wreck.'

'I could stop watching the news...'

He smiled.

'I could turn off my phone, practise meditation…' She looked up to his smile. 'And be all calm and serene and *How was your day, dear?* when you get home.'

'You wouldn't last five minutes…' Alistair sighed. 'Look, we went out once, and then shared four incredible days on your sofa-bed. It was great and then…not. That's okay. There's no need for a row or whatever.'

'I'd like a row,' Libby said. Because she wanted to shout out that she had made a mistake, and that she wished for him to go back to being upset at how much she'd hurt him. 'I want you to believe me.'

'But I don't, though,' he said. 'And that's not the best basis to start anything, is it?'

'No…' Libby had to concede. She did hate his job, his bike… He didn't believe that she'd changed her mind…

Alistair was right. It wasn't a great place to start.

'The thing is—' Libby stopped herself. Not because of pride, but because she just didn't know how to explain things—and it had nothing to do with the bang to her head.

It was simply that she didn't know how to explain that she didn't feel as if they were at the start of anything. She felt as if the start had been a very long time ago, and now they were in the *middle* of something.

She *had* fallen.

But not just down an escalator.

Libby was rather certain she had fallen straight in love.

That was what had terrified her.

And now it saddened her—more than she knew how to deal with.

'Alistair, I've been very spoilt, and I'm incredibly grateful, but I'm so much better that I feel like a bit of a fraud now.'

'You're not a fraud,' Alistair said. 'But you definitely seem better today. Look, you don't have to rush off. If you want to have a couple of days here while you're feeling better—a practice run, if you will—then you're welcome to stay. I'll be working twelve-hour shifts, so you won't even see me. Maybe go before I start my nights? Whatever works for you...'

'I could go shopping for you,' Libby offered. 'On my practice run.'

'No need. I've got a delivery coming tomorrow.'

'Well, I'll put it away.'

'It's all taken care of. Chloe does all that when I'm working.'

'Chloe?'

'The cleaner who went shopping for bed linen and such.'

'Oh.'

While she had known that his life was ordered, Libby felt she was being kept at arm's length—being silently told that he really didn't need or want her in his life.

At all.

The conversation had become strained, so his cobalt blue door was welcoming when it appeared.

And the little pot of earth by his door had tiny shoots emerging.

'Oh, look!' Libby said.

'Daffodils.'

Spring was around the corner, only it didn't feel like it for Libby.

The creak in the stairs as she walked up had grown familiar and it made her smile sadly. She was intending to change out of her damp jeans and his huge jumper, but as she headed for her room she turned and saw the door to his was open.

A suitcase was on the floor, and it was clear he was getting ready for his training course.

It made her feel hollow and empty, rather than scared as to the nature of his work.

She pulled on her tartan pyjamas and then went down to the kitchen and peered into his cupboards, wondering if she should offer to cook.

'Hungry?' he asked as he came into the room and found her staring into his fridge.

'I was about to offer to make dinner.'

'Well, good luck with that, because I haven't got anything in.'

'That's not very efficient of you,' she teased, because he was the most organised person in the world. 'What happened to your system?'

'You did,' Alistair said. 'We can order something in. What do you fancy?'

You, she was so tempted to say. But instead she pouted as she remembered no flirting was allowed.

Not standing by the fridge. *Especially* not standing by the fridge.

'Let me get dinner,' Libby said, taking her phone from her pyjama pocket.

And because it was Alistair, there were no arguments.

She ordered curry and extra garlic naans—because she didn't have to worry about end-of-the-night kisses and such.

It was a lazy evening, and there was a good film on television. Unfortunately, all too soon, it showed a couple making love on-screen.

'Awkward!' Libby gave a little laugh.

Alistair smiled, and Libby knew it was because she tended to mention the things most people would politely ignore.

But it was extremely awkward—watching a sex scene on TV whilst you were sitting next to the person you wanted to have sex with, but who no longer wanted to have sex with you.

He took up their plates.

'I'll do it,' Libby offered.

'It's fine,' Alistair said. 'I'm going to load the dishwasher, then I've got one more lecture to watch.'

'What time are you working tomorrow?'

'Midday to midnight…'

'I'll see you in the morning, then.'

Libby smiled, but it wavered as he turned without responding and went through to the kitchen.

They were over.

They were completely and utterly over.

Libby knew it, but she wished desperately that it wasn't so.

CHAPTER EIGHT

SHE WOKE TO the sound of Alistair in the shower.

It was late—almost eleven! She'd slept for twelve hours straight, but it felt worth it because, aside from a broken heart, she felt well. She felt so well, in fact, that she no longer suited her invalid status.

Really, it was time to pack her things and go…and get past the first day of really missing him.

Seriously missing him.

For. The. Rest. Of. Her. Life.

She didn't want to go.

Was it love? Libby pondered, wishing he'd hurry up so she could go to the loo. And, if it was, shouldn't she therefore fight for it? Shouldn't she force that row so they could move past it?

Only he didn't want one—and now neither did she.

She just wanted to touch him and say sorry with her body.

And thank you.

Just one kiss and they'd go back to the way they were, she was sure.

Shouldn't she at least try?

The old Libby would have.

And the old Libby, she decided, was back.

She and Alistair had an unvoiced agreement. After the first couple of days, when he'd waited outside, he now went downstairs and remained down there while she showered, and Libby did the same for him. Also, if she was in her bedroom when he showered, she remained in there.

But not this morning!

Perhaps she should be grateful for the ugly tartan pyjamas, given that the house was freezing, but they weren't exactly seductive. Very deliberately she avoided the mirror, not wanting to see her fluffy hair and lose confidence in herself…

She opened up the bedroom door and glanced down the hall. She wanted to slip into his bed and surprise him, but she decided that might be a bit much.

She started as the bathroom door opened.

He was naked except for a towel wrapped

around his slim hips, and he paused at the un-expected sight of her.

Her eyes drank him in. Fresh from the shower. His thick, dark hair was damp, and a few drops of water still clung to his skin.

She wanted to lick them off.

His jaw was so smooth. There was a little bit of shaving cream by his ear, and she wanted to kiss that off too!

She looked at the sexy mouth that had had her blushing since it had mouthed *Long fall* at her. Her face felt as if it was on fire now.

Her whole body was.

Cotton wool hair or not, she knew there was sex in the air. She could feel it as she lifted her eyes from his mouth and finally, *finally*, met his.

He gave her one slow, searing glance that almost burned her skin and had her about to stumble over to him, but then, a second later, an indifferent expression shuttered his eyes. He gave her a curt nod, then strode down the hall, heading for the privacy of his bedroom.

He didn't say a word—just turned when he reached his room and gave her a stark warn-ing look. It was an accusatory glare that sent her stumbling into the bathroom, as if that had been her intention all along.

They both knew it hadn't been.

She heard him close his door firmly behind him. Shutting her out. As if she hadn't already got the message.

God, but he wanted her.

He had all along.

He'd wanted to give in on holding back, but he had told himself when he'd brought her to his home that he would not be taking advantage of their forced proximity, nor of the fact that Libby had been unwell.

Only, she was better now.

That had been no accidental bump into each other in the hall, Alistair thought as he sprayed deodorant and pulled on his uniform.

He had felt her longing fighting and tangling with his own from down the hall.

'Damn you, Libby,' he cussed, because he wanted her out of his home so he had space to think.

It was hard to think clearly when the person you needed to think about was in your home, sitting on your floor eating curry, lying in bed in the room next to you, relaxing on your sofa…

The woman who'd dumped him…who'd not even replied to his card… Of *course* she'd seen it before; he was not going to fall for that one. She'd turned his life inside out and upside down, and she was everywhere, and he needed her to be gone so he could think.

Yet he wanted her here.

Here, Alistair thought as he sat on his bed and did up his boots.

He wanted her here in his bed.

Aside from all that, he was late for work!

For her sins, there was no breakfast in bed for Libby.

In fact, she rather had the feeling he'd gone to work without having breakfast himself, because just a few moments later he'd gone down the stairs and she'd heard the front door close and then the sound of his bike.

His rejection stung—but she had seen desire in his eyes. Such desire that it somehow inspired her. Made her feel a little bit of hope that they maybe weren't quite done.

Was there still a chance?

Libby pondered the question as she made her bed, unsure whether she should strip it and pack.

She was well enough to go—she felt much more like her normal self now. Well, apart from the fact she was making her bed on rising, which she rarely did at home!

She was upset to find the kettle cold, because

that meant that he hadn't even had a cup of tea in his haste to get out of there.

Time to go, Libby.

It was nice, though, to have a little practice run of being alone and doing normal things. She made a bowl of cornflakes, and some toast and tea, and wondered if he'd mind if she pinched the poppy tray, because it was so pretty and so feminine...

Yikes. She'd bet it was one of his exes who had bought it.

She ate at the table and looked out onto his garden—which, unlike the house, looked a little neglected.

Perhaps she could offer to take his daffodils while he was away, Libby thought. It seemed such a shame that they would flower unseen.

Though of course really she was just trying to come up with an excuse to see him after he'd completed his course.

Returning his daffodils would be a good excuse...

But surely she could come up with something better than that?

She was rinsing her plate when she was startled by the sound of a key in the door. She jumped, in the hope that he was home, and then sagged when she recalled that he'd said Chloe, his cleaner, was coming.

'Hi, I'm just in here,' Libby called, and then smiled as Chloe came into the kitchen. 'I didn't want to startle you.'

Although it was actually Libby who felt startled—because Chloe was completely stunning.

Her caramel hair was tied high in a messy bun. She had legs right up to her neck, and she wore black tights with shorts over them and a jumper cinched with a belt. If Libby wore the same outfit she'd look as if she was playing dress-up, but it looked fantastic on Chloe.

'Startle me?' Chloe frowned at Libby's choice of words. 'Why would you?'

And with that she made it clear to Libby that she wasn't the first overnight guest to be found rinsing her plate in Alistair's kitchen.

'Anyway,' Chole said, 'I never know if he's on nights, so I don't call out...'

She stomped upstairs and returned a short while later with armfuls of navy linen—presumably from Alistair's bed, though Libby had never so much as seen it—and threw them into the washing machine, then slammed the door closed.

Disconcertingly, for Libby, Chloe made no further attempt at conversation.

She discarded the scarf, jumper and belt quite quickly, and was soon wearing just a very little vest top. She began emptying the dishwasher.

'How long have you worked—?' Libby tried.

Chloe turned and pointed to her headphones. 'I'm listening to my music.' She took one bud out. 'What did you want?'

'Nothing…'

Libby felt awkward, so she went through to the lounge, but Chloe soon came in there so that didn't help. She really was the sexiest cleaner ever. But she scowled at Libby as she vacuumed—so much so that Libby went and hid in the bedroom while the online shopping was delivered.

Her phone pinged, and her heart leapt when she discovered it was a text from Alistair. Despite rejecting her this morning, Alistair had dutifully texted to ask how she was, because it was her first day alone. He really was perfect.

She quickly replied.

Hiding from Chloe. She hates me.

Alistair called her. 'What's wrong?'

'I was joking—well, sort of. But she doesn't like me. It makes me think that she might like *you*.'

'Chloe?' he checked. 'No. That was ages ago—we were never serious.'

'So you two *have* been on with each other?' Libby's mouth gaped and she knelt up on the bed. 'Jesus, Alistair, you could have warned me. I'd have gone out, or…'

She was indignant, jealous and embarrassed all at the same time—even if it wasn't actually her place to be. It felt like her place, though.

'You're cross with me over Doughnut Man, yet you're sleeping with your cleaner.'

'It was a couple of times last summer. Look, I've got to go. I'm not discussing my private life while I'm at work.'

'Have you got a patient with you?'

'No.'

'Then you can answer my question. If we had made it back to your house as lovers, would you have warned me then?'

'Warned you?'

'Warned me that your sexy cleaner gets between your sheets. No wonder she doesn't shout out when she arrives. Does she just slip into your bed?'

'You don't get to ask that, Libby.'

'The one time I make my bed…' Libby knew that Chloe had assumed Libby was sleeping with Alistair. 'I'm really, *really* cross, Alistair.'

'Then you're being ridiculous!'

'Not on this occasion! And my anger has

nothing to do with my injury. You're an arrogant, insensitive prick—and when I say that I can pretty much guarantee I'm speaking on behalf of Chloe too.'

This time it was *she* who hung up on *him*. Then Libby got dressed and grabbed her bag and his spare key.

As she headed out, Chloe was sulkily pulling the sheets out of the washing machine, and Libby knew she wasn't misreading the situation. She was cross again, for both herself and Chloe, and so she went out.

She would come back once Chloe was gone, and then she would pack her things and leave, Libby decided as she walked down the street. She would like to have stomped, like Chloe, but she was too scared of slipping, so instead she took a few cleansing breaths and found they actually helped.

God, she was jealous.

What had gone on between him and Chloe wasn't any of her business, and that was a horrible thing to know.

When she got to the canal she managed a small laugh as the green-eyed monster faded into a blush and then cooled, and when she got to the café she caught her reflection in the mirror and saw she was back to her normal pink colour rather than pale.

After first checking that she had her bag and purse with her, Libby went in. The table she and Alistair had shared previously was taken by a couple far more loving couple than they had been when seated there. They were feeding each other pancakes and holding hands.

She wanted Alistair to hold her hand again.

'What can I get you?' the waiter asked.

There was actually nothing on the menu that she fancied, but she ordered anyway. 'Could I have a cheese and pickle sandwich...with lettuce, please?'

'Sure.'

'And crisps.'

She ordered tea too.

The same lovely lunch Alistair had made her.

It was soon served, and it was absolutely beautiful, with a glass teapot, and crisps on a plate rather than in a bag. But there were no chocolate biscuits for her to enjoy later.

Gosh, he had taken such care of her, even while feeling hurt and angry.

He had taken such care of her at every turn.

So, no, she wasn't leaving in a temper—but she would still pack this evening and be in bed by the time he got home. Tomorrow she would thank him, and then she would go back to her own flat.

The hardest part? How to say goodbye? With grace?

It was no one's fault but hers, Libby was sure.

Alistair wasn't so sure that everything was Libby's fault, though. After she hung up on him, it was he who was doubting *his* part in all this.

He wasn't even sleeping with Chloe. That had been over ages ago.

It wasn't the same as Doughnut Man, he thought angrily. Libby had gone out on a date a week after their break-up.

But she had never made it there, he reminded himself.

Had Libby really changed her mind about seeing him?

Did it even matter whether she had or not?

He stared at the phone, thinking of his own refusal to see her side of things.

'Hey,' Brendan said as he came over. 'What's up?'

'Nothing,' Alistair snapped.

Certainly he would not be discussing this with Brendan.

Later in the afternoon, he saw Brendan glance at him. 'How's Libby doing?' he asked.

'They kept her in for a couple of nights. Concussion.'

'I know that,' Brendan said. 'I meant, how has she been since discharge?'

'How the hell would I know?' Alistair said, still refusing to bring his private life in to work.

But it was a hopeless task. They all knew. The pick-up point for the cab home when Libby had been discharged from The Primary had been near the ambulance bay, and half the station seemed to have been lined up there.

Watching.

No doubt later gossiping.

Brendan soon confirmed that fact. 'I thought that was why you moved your leave? Because she went home with you?'

'No, I took her back to her flat,' Alistair corrected.

'Really?' Brendan checked as he started up the ambulance's engine. 'You left her there alone?'

Alistair said nothing.

'That's not like you...'

Alistair stared ahead.

'That was a pretty nasty head injury,' Brendan persisted. 'I would have thought that you, of all people—'

'She wanted to go home,' Alistair interjected—

and then gave in. 'But obviously that couldn't work. She's staying at mine for now.'

Brendan said nothing, but Alistair could feel his questions hanging in the silence.

'In the guest room,' he added.

They did a couple of straightforward jobs, but Alistair would have far preferred they'd been complex and something he could have really got lost in, because the evening dragged on slowly. There was just too much time to think.

'Are you looking forward to your course?' Brendan asked.

'I am.' Alistair nodded, but then thought for a moment. 'Although there's a lot to sort out before I head off...'

'Yeah, I heard there's a lot of pre-study.'

Alistair had done all the pre-study, and the lectures, and his packing would take no time at all. Yet it still felt as if there was an awful lot to sort out before he disappeared for six weeks.

Away from Libby's witchery, and the spell she had cast, he was able to think clearly for the first time in a while.

It wasn't just her angry words this afternoon that were replaying in his mind, but their conversation by the canal. She'd told him about the motorbike fatality that morning, and how it had scared her. Then she'd found out about his new job... As well as worrying about the medical investigations she was going through.

He'd been so cross about her method of getting over him—had felt so let down that she'd been going out on a date when she'd had her accident—that he hadn't really addressed *why* she had ended things in the first place.

It *wasn't* the same as his father rejecting him because of his career-change.

Libby had run in fear.

Fear of losing him.

He'd had that same sense of fear on the night she'd fallen. It had overridden everything—so much so that he'd done his best to put aside the hurt and anger...so much so that she was currently in his home.

'I was watching a lecture last night,' he said, looking over to Brendan and lying through his teeth.

He hadn't been watching a lecture last night. He'd been eating curry and resisting Libby. He just wanted, possibly needed, Brendan's thoughts. The man was in a brilliant marriage after all.

'It was called *Fight, Flight, Freeze...*'

'There's plenty more Fs,' Brendan said, and glanced over as if assessing him. 'You fight... you face things...'

'Not always.'

He looked out at the dark, gloomy streets. Libby, Alistair knew, always went into flight mode. Not at work—there she dealt with things with her own brand of humour—but in her private life she ran. And who could blame her?

He'd said she was like her mother, and in all the nice ways she was, but Helen Bennett just fell apart...

No wonder Libby found it difficult to talk about the problems in her private life.

Perhaps they did need to talk about it?

Or should he wait until after the course... when she was completely better?

It was odd, because he'd spent all this week thinking they wouldn't be able to last a single night apart. Now he knew that those feelings would still be there at the end of his course.

He didn't want to leave without sorting this out.

They were heading back to base and it was nearing midnight when Alistair decided he might need a bit more advice from Brendan— because he was actually considering knocking on Libby's bedroom door and asking to discuss things with her when he got home.

Fat chance of discussing things, though, he thought, as he recalled the burn of their chemistry this morning.

If she was still at his home.

If she hadn't returned to her flat in anger.

Libby had been so angry when he'd called, and he knew she was well enough to go home.

God, he hoped she was still at his place.

He'd wanted her to stay. He'd wanted her to finally be well enough so that they could speak about what had happened between them. Only the days seemed to have raced away, and now there was the drama of Chloe—who had never felt like a drama until now. Alistair held himself to high standards and had never cheated in his life.

A text came through from Chloe, telling him she wouldn't be working for him any more.

Damn.

Then a call came in, and it was clear there would be no getting home just after midnight. Instead of signing off, they were being dispatched to a gentleman with back pain who had been waiting for an ambulance for some considerable time.

As Brendan turned at a roundabout, Alistair looked over to his colleague. 'Hey, Brendan, if you occasionally slept with someone…'

'I've only ever slept with my wife,' Brendan said proudly.

'You're no help, then.'

'Try me.'

'Okay.'

Unfortunately, he'd barely got past the description of his casual relationship with Chloe, and how that had been over ages ago, when the radio started to get busy.

They were just pulling in to their patient's house when Control contacted them again.

'Have you made patient contact?' they were asked—which was perhaps the first ominous sign that there was something big going on, because once contact had been made they couldn't be pulled from a job.

They hadn't made contact, though, and neither would they—for they were needed elsewhere.

Another call came over the radio then, and another, and another...

'Doesn't sound good,' Brendan said.

There was no more personal talk. Instead, they listened to the unfolding horror as they turned on the siren and made their way rapidly to the scene.

There would be no getting home on time and no talking to Libby tonight.

Alistair glanced at the time and saw it was almost midnight. He hoped to God that she was already in bed...hoped that Libby was oblivious to the hell he and Brendan were approaching.

* * *

It was one of those nights when people were just turning the television off before heading to bed, or closing down their computers, or hitting the *Do Not Disturb* button when a breaking news alert halted them. In Libby's case, she had packed all her things into her bag—although it had taken her far longer to do so than it had taken Alistair.

She wanted to be safely in bed, asleep, when he got home, as she knew he'd be worn out, and she wasn't sure she could manage to say she was leaving tomorrow and thank him without bursting into tears, or something equally pathetic.

She was still working on that graceful goodbye.

Her brain was back in worry mode, and it felt good to be herself again.

Perhaps she could leave a note? Though it might be better to wait until she was home, and from there send a present and card.

Send it to where, though? He would be away on his course for the next six weeks.

Or should she put her heart on the line and tell Alistair that she loved him?

Libby stood in the guest room—when she really wanted to be in his—and looked at her bag which she had so reluctantly packed.

Everything about tonight felt wrong.

Go to bed, Libby, she told herself, changing into her tartan pyjamas.

Alistair's laundry service had stopped a couple of days ago—she was well enough to do her own laundry now.

They were the same clothes she'd been wearing this morning.

Reject me again, then! Libby thought, as she buttoned them up. *But I am going to tell you I love you!*

Or should she go to bed instead?

Remembering she'd left the heating on, Libby padded down the stairs and turned it off—but now she was back to worrying about everything! Should she turn it back on and keep the house warm for him?

She was trying to decide when her phone pinged and she frowned at the news alert.

She tried to discard it, telling herself it must be wrong.

An exaggeration.

Probably nothing.

But then another alert chimed, and it was more specific this time.

Reports Confirmed...

City of London...

He'd be nowhere near there, Libby told herself, as she saw that it was just after midnight. His shift was over and he was probably on his way home.

Even so, she turned on the television and had to then work out how to operate his remote to get to the news.

And straight away she knew that the situation wasn't being exaggerated.

London was in trouble tonight.

Her hands were shaking so much that she couldn't work out how to adjust the volume for quite a while.

No.

Oh, no.

No, no, no.

Yes.

It was one of those awful nights where you don't go to bed. Instead you watch and feel ill and really kind of hate the world—or rather its inhabitants, and the awful things they do to each other at times.

Libby sat on the edge of sofa or paced, watching in horror while also keeping one ear open, hoping for the purr of his motorbike as it turned into the street and no doubt annoyed the neighbours.

As much as she hated his bike, she'd give anything to hear it right now.

But it never arrived.

A major incident had been declared, and if she hadn't been off sick she might well have been called in to work. Instead, she flicked through the channels and tried to get more news on her phone. She read that there were now unconfirmed reports of two emergency personnel injured.

She tried to keep calm and drank tea.

An awful lot of tea.

Then she burst into tears, remembering the cold kettle this morning and how Alistair had gone to work without tea.

'That'll be you...' Brendan said to Alistair as they arrived on scene and watched the Tactical Response Vehicles moving into the warm zone

They were being held back in the cold zone, as it was an extremely active crime scene and casualties would be brought out to them.

'There's a way to go before that,' Alistair said.

Their conversation was not stilted, but there were large gaps between sentences as they listened to the radio and watched the unfolding scene in silence.

'Will Alison be waiting up?' Alistair asked.

'Yes.'

'Should you call her?'

'No need,' Brendan said, pausing as the police moved a barricade and they inched their ambulance a few feet ahead.

'She'll be worried if she's up, though...' Alistair frowned.

'Of course she will be,' Brendan said. 'That's part of the job, isn't it?'

He said it so matter-of-factly, as if it was simply a matter of course, and it dawned on Alistair then that he'd never had a significant other to worry about.

He'd never had to do this job with someone worrying about him at home.

'Libby's probably asleep,' Alistair said, and realised he had named her to Brendan as the one person he was thinking of tonight. 'Otherwise there'd be a hundred missed calls.'

He looked at his phone and hoped to God that he was right and Libby had no idea what was going on.

They sat for hours, watching and waiting to help. Alistair just wanted to be in there—right in the thick of it—because it was hell being held back. Instead, he kept thinking of himself and Libby walking along the canal, and how he'd dismissed her concerns for his safety.

'We had a bit of a disagreement,' Alistair said, thinking back to this afternoon and how cross she had been. 'I was going to talk to her about it when I got home…' He looked at his phone, still debating whether to text and risk waking her.

'Alison and I have a deal,' Brendan said.

'What's that?'

'I never leave for work on a row.'

Alistair stared ahead, less than soothed by the fact that he and Libby had never had that row. Oh, at first it had been for all the right reasons, but in recent days it had been nothing but wounded pride holding him back.

He thought back to this morning.

They could have made love, and instead he'd walked away and closed the door on her.

'I don't need to call her because nothing's been left unsaid,' Brendan nattered on, and where he once might have sounded smug in his marital bliss, to Alistair right now Brendan sounded wise.

Everything between him and Libby had been left unsaid.

But Brendan didn't get to finish his recipe for wedded bliss, because there was the sudden sound of rapid gunfire, followed by a pounding on the ambulance, and it took a second for them both to register that their vehicle was under attack.

'Get back!'

The police were waving their arms and

shouting, and the bricks or bottles that were hammering the vehicle disappeared as Brendan swiftly reversed. Then the rear doors opened, and for split-second Alistair did not know whether or not they were being invaded.

'GSW to the neck!' he heard.

It was a female police officer, literally dragging in a colleague, and Alistair got straight to work.

'Good man,' he said, as the young policeman pressed a cloth to his own wound while his colleague did all she could to assist.

That his bleeding wasn't arterial was the only reason the patient was alive.

New crime scenes were being established, and their ambulance was now considered part of the hot zone. It was the most volatile situation Alistair had ever been in. There were still missiles being aimed at the ambulance, even as Brendan skilfully backed them further out. The policewoman pressed on her colleague's wound now, as Alistair administered oxygen and secured an IV. She helped squeeze through fluids as Alistair did all he could to keep his patient alive while Brendan alerted the nearest hospital.

'Gunshot wound to neck,' Brendan told them. 'GCS?' he called to Alistair, wanting more information.

'Was twelve—now nine,' Alistair called back, and relayed the young policeman's deteriorating vials.

In the moments just preceding his limbs had become flaccid, his eyes were no longer opening, and he was making no attempt to vocalise now. The only sound coming from the patient was the ringing of his phone in his jacket—a loved one, Alistair was sure, desperate to know he was safe.

When they arrived, the hospital was in full major incident mode, and the patient was rushed through to the experts waiting to receive him. But there was no time to follow this patient. They were already being summoned back…

As Libby waited for the kettle to boil, she tried to tell herself that Alistair was surely fine—and that what was happening tonight was the reason she could not let herself love him.

Except it was a ridiculous argument because she already did.

She already loved him.

It was like a baptism of fire, Libby told herself.

Excuse the dreadful pun, she told herself as she walked into the lounge and an awful image came on the screen.

'In further developments,' the reporter said, 'emergency vehicles are now coming under attack...'

Oh, God...stay calm, stay calm.

They all had to.

Alistair had to.

So she would too.

But when she wasn't at work she was dreadful at it, and she watched in horror as the news got worse and worse...

It would be unfair to call him with her hysterics now—though of course she'd be directed to leave a voicemail.

Would it be too much to text him? Just so she could have the opportunity to say *I love you*? Libby pondered. Or rather *I love you, I love you, I love you, I love you, I love you, I love you, I love you, I love you...* Maybe five hundred times over—which was strange because she hadn't yet said it once...

All that tea meant a lot of dashes upstairs to the loo. And on one trip came the dreadful thought that she hadn't even seen inside his bedroom.

It was wrong, perhaps, but given the scary circumstances Libby decided she was going to cross boundaries.

She pushed open the pale wooden door and turned on the light.

Dark curtains were closed and the navy sheets that had in part caused their row this afternoon had been replaced by willow-green ones and a matching cover.

The wooden floorboards were softened by a dark rug, and the suitcase she had only seen from the hall still lay on the floor, one side filled with folders and manuals, the other waiting to be filled with clothes.

Lucky the patients who had him, Libby thought.

Why, oh, why hadn't she waited until she'd calmed down when she'd found out about his new work?

Why had she raced in and ended things?

Because she was as impulsive as he was sensible…

So impulsive that she was tempted again to peel off her tartan pyjamas and climb into his bed and wait for him there.

Hardly a dignified exit!

And not the graceful goodbye she had been practising all afternoon.

And anyway, she had denied them both her right to do that.

Now she was a guest in his home.

An inconvenience foisted upon him.

The user of newly bought guest towels.

She thought of his words on the night he'd

brought her back to her flat after her stay in the hospital. *'You dumped me. You don't get to share a bed with me.'*

And how he'd rather miss a nail-biting football match to load the dishwasher and head upstairs than get cosy with her.

Tears threatened to come. So she did the right thing and turned off the light and walked out. She padded downstairs and watched as the police stormed a building and shattering noises caused the tears to come tumbling from her eyes.

She felt a desperate need to get fresh air, despite being in no danger herself.

She opened up the front door and gulped in icy lungsful of fresh, cold air. She peered up at the dark sky and then down to the pot of daffodils that were still only shoots. She could not bear it that they might flower unseen, and that had a far darker meaning now, as she forced herself to face the stark reality that he might never return.

She scanned the street for the lights of his bike, willing him to come home.

Nothing.

Then finally it was over.

Libby stood in the lounge as the reporter informed her that the situation was now under control, though the breaking dawn would be met with breaking hearts for too many. The world was a crueller place, and London was grey in the silence of the morning.

And still she didn't know how he was, or whether she was overreacting, or how she was even supposed to be...

All Libby knew was that she loved him.

Then she jumped as she saw there was a police car pulling up outside. She gave a cry of relief when she saw Alistair getting out.

She fled upstairs to her bed and still did not know how to be.

Was it even her place to be upset?

Should she pretend to be asleep, as if she hadn't seen it and been up all night worrying? Or should she smile and casually enquire, *How was your night?* Or should she wish him good morning and pack her bags and walk out?

Because maybe she'd been right all along and she simply wasn't up to being in love with someone who did this kind of job? Someone who was actively trying to be present at this type of scenario on every scale.

She heard his footsteps on the stairs and did not know if he would head straight for his bedroom or not. Did he even know there was frantic love burning behind the door of the guest room of his home?

She wanted to shout out to him, to run to

him, to drape herself around him in relief. But perhaps that wasn't what he needed after such a night.

Then the door to her room was pushed open without a warning knock, and she was too late to close her eyes and pretend to be asleep.

'Hey.'

He was at the door, and though he was often pale after a long shift, this morning he was as white as a ghost.

'How are you?' he asked.

'Fine,' Libby said in a rather high voice. 'How are you?'

'Fine,' Alistair said.

'That's good.'

She stared at his drained, exhausted face and knew she did not want to foist her tumbled emotions on him.

'What did you do last night?' he asked.

'Me?' Libby said. 'Oh, the usual. I watched a film on my laptop with a bar of chocolate and then I dozed off...' she lied, playing for time as she floated in sheer relief that he was safely home.

'What film did you watch?'

It was such an odd thing to ask, given the night he had surely had, but perhaps he just wanted to speak about something normal. Or possibly he was testing her, seeing if she'd had

the mettle to stay calm or had instead been
frantically pacing the floor.

Which she had been, of course.

Wuthering Heights.' Another lie, of course,
but it was a very safe lie, given that she knew
the film back to front and inside out as she
had watched it so very many times—not that
Alistair could possibly know.

'Oh?'

'It was actually quite good.'

'Quite good?' he enquired.

'Mmm…' she said. 'I remember reading the
book at school.'

Alistair loved how hard she was trying to lie.

He loved everything about getting to come
home to her: the mugs on the coffee table in
the lounge…the balls of tissues too.

He knew that she must have leapt into bed
when he'd arrived home. Not only had he seen
the twitch of the lounge curtains, he had also
felt the warmth of her being downstairs, while
it was cold up here. There was no silver foil
from a chocolate bar, and her bed was far too
neat for a night spent beneath its covers. The
curtains hadn't even been closed…

'Although,' Libby mused, elaborating upon
her lie, as if she really had been tucked up in
bed with chocolate and watching the film on

her computer last night, 'there was a part that wasn't quite as I'd have played it…'

His lips wanted to twitch into a smile. After a night spent in hell it was so nice to step out of it for a moment, to be here rather than out there. So he lingered in her will-o'-the-wisp world for a moment longer. He wanted more of the light she brought to his life.

'What do you mean, it wasn't how you'd have played it? I'm not with you.'

'I mean, if I were the actress playing Cathy I'd have done it differently…' Her green eyes met his.

'How so?' he asked.

'You know the part when Cathy says, "I am Heathcliff"?'

'No,' he said. 'Not off-hand. What about it?'

'When I read the book at school—*ages* ago—I seem to remember that I imagined Cathy declaring it loudly, but in the film she says it quietly.'

'The film you were watching last night?'

'Yes.'

'How would you have played it?'

He was dying to know, and of course Libby obliged.

She leant forward. 'This is how she went…' Libby dropped her voice so she was soft-spoken. '"I am Heathcliff…" Whereas I think it should have been more...' she knelt up and spread out her arms '...more adamant. "I *am* Heathcliff..."'

It was a burst of pure emotion and it was aimed only at him.

'Actually, I think she should have risen to stand...' she did the very same, '...and loudly declared, *"I. Am. Heathcliff!"'*

Libby almost toppled over with the effort of her own performance and he caught her.

'I believe you,' he said, and pulled her off the bed and into his arms.

'Please don't. Because I'm lying...'

And then she was kissing his cold, cold face, and he was holding her so tight, and he didn't seem to mind the kisses she rained upon him.

'I haven't been watching the film! I just know it back to front, inside out...'

'I meant, I believe you that you would be foolish enough to turn around and try to walk down an escalator—and, yes, I believe you that you don't check your post. I mean, clearly you do stand on the bed...'

'I do!' She was guilty as charged, and happily so, now that he finally believed her. 'I'm so, so glad you're home.'

She rested her head on his wide shoulder and breathed him in, just nestled her head there in the best place to be, as he turned and kissed her cheek. It was a small, tender kiss that tasted of the tears she'd been crying, which she had tried not to reveal.

'I'm so relieved you're home.'

'I know,' Alistair said as he held her. 'Last night I thought a lot about how you were feeling, and I decided that I'm a selfish bastard to do this job and not consider the impact—'

'No, no, no! I'm neurotic.'

'Never change,' he said.

'Nor you.'

'Do you want to see my bedroom?'

'I peeked last night.'

He carried her into his bedroom and pulled back the sheet and placed her in his bed. But she had so many questions.

'Why did the police bring you home, Alistair?'

'Because I asked them to,' he said as he undid his boots. It seemed to her a very long time since he'd put them on. 'I went to check on a patient I'd brought in…a colleague of theirs.'

'How were they?'

'Just out of Theatre,' Alistair said. 'Alive. To be honest, I didn't think he would be, and nor did his partner.' He was quiet for a moment. 'Anyway, I said to her it would be so stupid to get killed on my way home after a shift like that and she gave me a lift.'

He turned and looked at Libby.

'Why do you have so many keys?'

Libby blinked. It seemed like such an odd question. 'I have Mum and Dad's. My car. My friend Olivia's, in case she gets locked out. The theatre at home...' She grimaced. 'I ought to give those back. Why do you want to know?'

'Because I want to know *you*.' He didn't look at her directly. 'I'll give up the bike, but not the job.'

'You don't have to—but thank you very much if you do,' Libby said. 'The only thing I *will* ask you to give up is your cleaner.'

'Done. Last night Chloe fired me,' he said. 'Although she texted this morning to check I was okay.'

'Grr...' Libby said, and then took a breath. 'Fair enough.' Then she looked at him, standing there, and her voice was serious. '*Are* you all right?'

'Yes.'

'Is Brendan?'

'He's okay. A few of us went for breakfast and had a bit of a debrief. Brendan's been great, actually. He gives good advice.'

'I'm pleased you can talk to him.' Libby took another breath, unsure if he wanted to discuss last night now. 'Do you want to—?'

'Not now,' he cut in. 'I want to sleep.' Then

he looked at her. 'How about you? Are you okay?'

'Yes,' Libby said.

She looked at him standing there. He seemed a bit stunned, really. She thought of the toll his job must take on him. Yet he took it so willingly. As well as that, he loved it—and she loved him, so that was that.

So, yes, she was okay, too, because she would far rather be here than anywhere else in the world.

And then he changed her world all over again.

'We're getting married,' Alistair said as he took off his uniform.

'Are we?' Libby smiled, not believing him for a moment, certain he must just be on some sort of post-dramatic night duty high.

'We are,' he affirmed, and his tone was so absolute, and his eyes so intent, that everything that had been shaking inside Libby since that first news alert had pinged in suddenly stilled.

'Married?' she checked.

'If you'll have me.'

She would marry him this second, right now, if she could, without hesitation or doubt.

It was Alistair's certainty she was scared to believe in.

Which was odd, because it was his very certainty that she relied upon.

She was scared of him retracting it later, when his common sense had invaded and he'd thought it through.

'Alistair…' She flailed, attempting to be the sensible one even when she didn't want to be! 'We've known each other…what? Three weeks? What happened to measure twice, cut once? Or look before you leap?'

'Is that a no?'

'Of course not. It's a complete yes from me. But what if I can't get pregnant? Or what if you're just feeling all messed up from last night…?'

'I'm incredibly clear *thanks* to last night,' Alistair corrected. 'I thought we had time on our side—that I'd find out about your jangly prison warder keys and such. I was hoping that we could maybe pick things up in six weeks… sort it out once you were well. I was starting to realise we'd still be feeling the same. And then last night showed me we might not have time, and also that this is love.'

Libby swallowed. His love was everything she craved—but not if it was just a knee-jerk response to last night's events. Not if it was just words that he might later come to regret.

'Alistair, I'm worried that you're—'

'Libby,' he cut in, 'whether or not I love you is one thing you *never* have to worry about.'

To a constant worrier, that was the nicest thing he could possibly say.

'When they rushed you off for your head CT I hated not being your next of kin. And I think, last night, you kind of *were* my next of kin...'

'I was. I am...' Not legally, perhaps, but they were the closest person to each other in the world, and she had held him in her heart all night.

He was the person she first and foremost needed to know, because his heart was beating in time with hers, because he would be there beside her even when he was physically distant.

This love took nothing from your love for others—it simply elevated one person to The One.

And the one she loved was climbing into bed, where he lay with his eyes closed as she slipped off her pyjamas and they rolled into each other. He felt like a block of ice, so cold that he made her thighs jerk when one of his legs slid in between hers and the other wrapped around her.

'Ow,' she said, because he really was cold, but she clamped her thighs around his all the same. Then, wrapped in each other, they let the horror of the night recede and return, then recede again, like the tide going out.

'Can you believe,' Alistair said sleepily, with his eyes closed, 'while all this was going on some bastard swiped my daffodils…?'

'Oh, that was me,' Libby readily admitted. 'I thought that if anything happened to you… Well, a condom box isn't much to show for things, so I decided I would be keeper of your daffodils.'

He gave a low laugh and opened his beautiful brown eyes to meet hers. 'You took them?'

'They're by my packed bag, in the wardrobe in the guest room.'

'You actually packed?'

'Extremely reluctantly.' Libby nodded. 'I've also stolen your poppy tray.'

'We'll unpack it all later,' Alistair said. 'And we'll sort out your flat…' He couldn't think of all the logistics right now. 'I don't know when…' He looked at her then. 'Are you going to be lonely for the next few weeks?'

'No,' Libby said, 'so long as I can sleep here.'

'Of course.'

And then she was serious, her heart still beating a little too wildly in an odd mixture of fears glimpsed and elation. And how lucky she was to be here.

'I wanted to text you last night and tell you I love you, but I didn't want to add to the strain of what was going on...'

'Thank you,' he said. 'I wanted to do the same, while at the same time I was hoping you were asleep.'

'No.' Libby shook her head. 'I think the fact that I love you has been my problem all along.'

'Loving me was the problem?'

'Yes.' It was hard to explain, but she tried. 'I didn't just fall in love with you, Alistair, I crashed into it. I dived into it. And when I came up for air, I didn't know what had happened. I couldn't explain it to myself, let alone to my friends. I don't expect you to understand—'

'Oh, but I do. Do you know why we stayed at yours for four days?' Alistair asked.

'Because we were too happy to move?'

'In part. But I had a feeling that once I brought you to my place, you would only ever go back to that flat to pack up your things and bring them here. For good. I needed to think. But being in your sofa-bed was too nice for me to do that. Then, when I got home, I still felt the same. So I called, asking you to come over. I knew how I felt about you. And then you dumped me.' He smiled a smile that told her all was forgiven. 'Seems I was right. You're here and you're not leaving.'

'Never,' Libby said as his hand moved down past her ribs to her hips, stroking her skin.

The warmth and togetherness of them was restorative. His touch sent a delicious shiver through her and her touching him did the same. His forearms, his flat stomach… She touched him lightly, so relieved he was there. She held him, stroked him, as they explored each other without haste. They stared at each other in the false night they had created by closing out the world.

The glitter in his eyes, the intensity of his stare, was something she had seen before, of that she was certain. And Libby knew she had been bathed in that same glow before. They really had loved each other, even then…

Their mouths met softly and they kissed in a slow kiss, huddled beneath the covers, their tongues teasing. His hand slid under her and then he pulled her right into him, his kiss rougher and more thorough.

And deeper too.

He rolled her, his kisses chasing her onto her back, and Libby relished the weight of him and how it felt to be pinned down by love. There was no need to hold back their constant desire and no feelings to resist.

And they really were tearing up their rule-books, because she parted for him readily, and he didn't even attempt to reach for protection.

Libby was so ready that when he squeezed in she moaned with bliss, her stomach curling as she arched her back.

His breath was hot in her ear. 'You feel so good...' he told her, moving slowly.

'So do you.'

Oh, he did. He felt so, so good.

He moved up on his forearms and his face was over hers. Libby reached with her mouth for his, but found his strong shoulder instead, and she tasted his salty skin as he glided and moved within her, taking her, driving her on, ever closer.

They moved together in a slow, deep rhythm and Libby tried to keep her eyes open, so she could see how he looked with his eyes closed in pleasure.

Then she felt a spread of heat the length of her spine, which he'd traced that first time, and it was Libby who closed her eyes. Even her hands tightened in tension. And then came the final swell of him, and his breathless shout that brought her home.

'Oh, Alistair...'

Her orgasm was fading, but the heat and the love and the emotion remained, and she cried on him just a little, in giddy relief that he was here.

'It's okay,' he said.

'I know it is.'

These were happy tears, and so they lay together, catching their breath, his hand stroking her arm. Coming back to the world together...

Alistair's phone was ringing, again and again.

'Turn it off,' Libby said.

He went to do so, but then he must have changed his mind because he started texting.

'Alistair!' She was affronted. 'How can you be on your phone when—?'

'It's from my father.' He showed her the message.

He had texted to say that he was proud of him.

'Oh...' She felt her eyes well with tears. 'Call him!'

'I've already spoken to him. He saw the news when he woke up and called me.'

'I'm so pleased.' Libby smiled, thinking how sometimes it took something terrible to happen, or almost happen, to wake people up and make them realise what was truly important in life.

'They want to meet you,' he said.

'Ooh…' Libby said. 'We really are doing this, aren't we?'

'We really are.'

And now poor Alistair really was having a time of it. Because when the phone rang, instead of checking the caller ID or the number, as he usually would, he answered it—only to find himself naked in bed and on a video call with her father.

'I've been trying to call Libby,' he said. 'You weren't caught up in that mess last night, were you?'

Then he must have recognised the curls on the pillow next to Alistair.

'What the hell…?'

It was Libby who rescued the situation. 'Dad!' She took the phone. 'Alistair and I are getting married, so you don't have to kill him. I love you and Mum so much, but he's had a dreadful night, so I have to go now…'

'But, Libby, you hardly know him.'

'I know that I love him,' Libby said. 'Kisses!' She turned off his phone. 'You have to marry me now.'

'I do.'

'I'm going to make you a cup of tea,' she said. 'Then we're going to sleep, and I might even go and get doughnuts later. How does that sound?'

'Perfect.'

Indeed it did.

EPILOGUE

'I THINK I'M in labour.'

Unusually, Alistair was running late for work, but of course he halted and turned around, even though Libby had said this *many* times before.

'Why do you think that?'

'I've got backache,' Libby told him, although admittedly she always thought that. 'Maybe the sex triggered it.'

'Could you perhaps have backache because you're thirty-six weeks pregnant?' Alistair suggested, stroking her very pregnant belly for a full ten minutes and feeling a couple of kicks but no contractions. 'Backache is normal, Libby.'

'I know it is, but…'

It had taken three years of trying, and now that their baby was soon to be here every day apart from it felt a day too long. Maybe her conviction that she was in labour really was just wishful thinking.

She looked up at him. 'Do you have to go to work?'

Of course he did.

She was the girl who cried wolf. Libby knew that as he gave her a kiss and headed off to dive into the underground.

This felt different, though.

Except the midwife at the hospital didn't sound concerned when she called a couple of hours later.

'No contractions?' the midwife checked.

'No.'

'And baby's moving?'

'A lot,' Libby agreed, watching a tiny foot push at her stomach.

'Your waters are intact?'

'They are.'

Given that in recent days she had called the hospital rather a lot, Libby already knew the questions the midwife would ask.

Everything was fine, she was reassured. In fact, the midwife pretty much said the same as Alistair had—that backache was normal, she had an antenatal appointment tomorrow, and she was to call back if anything changed.

Nothing changed.

Her mum called, and Libby airily said that

all was well. 'I'm not due for another four weeks,' Libby said. She certainly didn't tell her about her backache.

Olivia called and patiently listened to her symptoms.

'We can't wait to come and see you when the baby is here,' she said.

Olivia had visited them only last week, with little Timothy. They'd stayed in the guest room and Alistair had happily babysat when she and Olivia went out. Possibly he'd agreed to it to get an evening's relative peace! Libby's new theatre group had decided on their next production…and it was *that* one. *The* one. And if Libby didn't get the leading lady part—well, she'd possibly die.

This morning, Libby updated her friend on the new production.

'They've announced the auditions,' she told Olivia. 'And they're holding them on the baby's due date. I'm sure it was done deliberately, so that I couldn't be there.'

'Libby!'

'No, I'm quite sure. Well, I don't care if I give birth mid-audition. I'm going to be there.'

'Oh, I'm sure you are!' Olivia laughed.

Libby found that she was pacing and unsettled, so she had a lovely long bath and wrapped herself in jade-green towels… Ha-ha! And then she thought about a morning snack, because apart from the baby and the auditions she thought about food more than anything else.

She got on with setting up her poppy tray, and caught sight of her reflection in the French windows. She was back to feeling like a duck again. Not because she felt drab and plain, just because of the way she was waddling around.

Libby thought back to the last time she'd compared herself to a duck—sitting in that café by the canal, so certain she'd blown things. So certain that it was all down to her, not knowing that Alistair was working it out too.

Always.

And then she stopped thinking about ducks and fond memories as her stomach tightened into a rock and pulled at her back.

If this was the start of labour, then she was getting an epidural.

'Does Libby think she's in labour again?' asked Trent, because Alistair's phone was buzzing *again*.

Alistair might be the new guy in the Tactical Response Unit, but they all knew about Libby and the upcoming birth!

Alistair listened to her symptoms.

'*One* contraction?' he checked.

'You can be *so* condescending,' Libby snarled, and hung up on him.

Her tone left him frowning.

Libby didn't snarl. Well, not often. Only when something serious was going on…

He called her straight back and was met with a shaky announcement.

'I'm in labour.'

'Okay,' he said. 'Tell me what's happening.'

'Alistair, my waters have just broken…' She started groaning.

'What?'

'You have to go because I need to call an ambulance. I want to push…'

'I'll call it in,' Alistair said. 'Libby, try not to push…' he attempted, but she'd already gone.

Oh, God…

Libby was thinking exactly the same!

Well, a slightly more exaggerated version!

Oh. My. God!

Another contraction gripped her, even stronger than the one before. So much so that she wasn't even able to make it into the hall to open the front door. Instead, she dropped to the floor by the washing machine.

But Alistair had called it in, and Libby got more than an ambulance.

She got Lina coming round the back via the

gate, then entering through the French doors of the kitchen.

'Hi, Libby.' Lina crouched down beside her and did a sweeping assessment. 'I'm going to open the front door and Brendan's getting all the equipment. Okay?'

Libby nodded.

And it wasn't just Brendan—there was the sound of a back-up crew arriving too.

As well as that, all the neighbours had come out to see what on earth was going on at number thirty-five!

And then Libby got a Tactical Response Vehicle too!

Alistair came charging down the hall and was treated to the sight of Brendan's back, in his kitchen, and Lina on her knees with Libby against the washing machine.

There was no delay button for this—Alistair could see the dark hair of his baby's head, already crowning!

'Told you I was in labour!' Libby accused, even as her arms simultaneously reached for him.

'You did,' Alistair agreed as he crouched down by her side.

'She's going to make you pay for this, mate,' Brendan said, 'for the rest of your life.'

'I know,' Alistair said, and kissed her very red face.

He looked over to Lina, who was about to deliver his baby, and she looked up at him with a quiet offer. Did he want to take over? But no… He was needed at the other end.

'Libby, listen to Lina,' he said. 'You're amazing…'

'Please can we call him—?'

'We are *not* calling him Heathcliff,' Alistair said. 'No matter how much you cry.'

'You really don't know what you're having?' Brendan enquired.

'We don't,' Libby said through gritted teeth.

Alistair did.

He'd cheated, and was very quietly confident that there would no need to deny Libby her dreadful choice of name for a boy…

'I'm scared,' Libby admitted through chattering teeth.

She was terrified, and yet so excited and so pleased that Alistair was there, holding her tight as she did her very best not to push, so their baby could make a slightly slower entrance than the one it wanted.

'Okay,' Lina said. 'Well done. The head's out…'

She was shivering, and too scared to look, so

she just breathed in Alistair's scent, and heard his heart thumping as fast as hers in his chest, and he didn't show, not for a second, that he was anything other than completely calm.

And then Libby gave a little sob as their baby was delivered.

She looked down at the beautiful dark-haired baby who lay sprawled on her stomach like a little washed-up frog.

'She's here!' Alistair said.

And Libby watched her baby turn pink as she stroked her stunned little face, then turned to Alistair and kissed the proud husband and father.

'She is...'

It hadn't been easy to get to this day—not easy at all. Some miracles took time. But finally here was their baby.

Libby heard a sound that she never had before—a single sob from Alistair.

He attempted recovery with a sniff, but then had to press his fingers in his eyes as his colleagues and friends all congratulated them.

'Catherine,' Alistair said, and very deftly cut the cord, enabling Libby to scoop their long-awaited and so very gorgeous baby right up to her.

Together they welcomed her to the world, touching her fingers and watching the curl of her toes, gazing into milky blue eyes as they blinked their first blinks and her rosebud mouth pursed.

'Is she breathing okay?' Libby asked, ever anxious.

It was their little girl who answered that.

Tiny, pink, squirmy and now cross, she opened her mouth and started letting out indignant screams, already searching to be fed.

'Cathy!' Libby cooed as she gazed upon her daughter.

'Catherine,' Alistair corrected again, and everyone else, including Libby, suppressed a smile.

All present knew that Alistair didn't have a hope of winning that one…

* * * * *

*If you enjoyed this story, check
out these other great reads from
Carol Marinelli*

Unlocking the Doctor's Secrets
The Nurse's Reunion Wish
The Midwife's One-Night Fling
Their One Night Baby

All available now!